SMITH AND JONES

He had files on both Smith and Jones—nice thick files, thicker than was normal for diplomats; dusty records of careers of indiscretion and drunkenness. Not at all the sort of men to be sent across the Iron Curtain, to be trusted with their country's secrets. But they had friends in high places who indicated that it might be best if he made allowances. Smith and Jones were trash, and he knew it—but perhaps it would be wise to swim with the tide.

When they defected he became the scapegoat. 'Jones isn't important,' Colonel Bellinger said. 'He's cultural. A cultural drunk. Films and pictures and books and booze. He knows nothing worthwhile. People like him are two a penny, and the price is just about right. . . . Smith *is* important. . . . He can talk a good deal, if he cares to. . . . And together, they're a propaganda gift, *your* gift. But you're going to get your gift returned. Or cancelled out. Or covered up.'

By nightfall he was on his way.

BY THE SAME AUTHOR

SIGNS OF THE TIMES

Smith And Jones
by Nicholas Monsarrat

CASSELL · LONDON

CASSELL & COMPANY LTD
35 Red Lion Square · London WC1
and at
MELBOURNE · SYDNEY · TORONTO
JOHANNESBURG · CAPE TOWN · AUCKLAND

———

Printed in Great Britain by
Ebenezer Baylis & Son Limited, The Trinity Press, Worcester
F. 263

One

MY nickname in the Foreign Service is 'The Drill-Pig'. It annoyed me when I first heard it, but it doesn't annoy me any longer. Let's say that I have risen above it. A long way.

It is a fact that about twenty years ago I was an army drill-instructor. It was, and is, a specialist job, designed to turn surly kids into the semblance of men. It is based on the army belief that if you shout at even the most worthless lout long enough and loud enough, he will become a soldier of sorts, good enough to die when you finally send him up front.

With hard cases, it can be a long process; hot and sweaty, a grimy endurance test for both sides. It is punitive. It has to be. For unless you bear down hard, and keep on doing so, individual heads get out of line, individual backbones waver. That is because their owners are not yet soldiers. They are still people, which is not the currency the army wants.

In those days, I did my share of barking and bearing-down. I must have stared back at ten thousand pairs of glazed or sullen eyes, straightened ten thousand spines, blistered ten thousand pairs of feet. I enjoyed it, because I wasn't running in any popularity contest; a love-token from the graduating class would not show on my pay-sheet, much less on my service record. The state of near-mutiny, the seething hatred, were all the tribute I needed, on or off the parade-ground. The end-product was soldiers, which was what I was paid to turn out.

Of course, a few weak sisters ended up as so-called nervous wrecks, only good enough to push a pen, or were discharged under the convenient label 'Lack of Moral Fibre'. I could always prove that they wouldn't have been any good anyway. A colleague once said that our job was to turn little bastards into big bastards. I would never quarrel with that.

But that is all a long time ago. Since then, I have graduated to a different part of the forest. Now you can call me a policeman, a Security man.

That is a specialist job, also. It remains punitive. But now, you can afford to do your shouting in whispers, you can keep order with different weapons, different kinds of needle. The kids knuckle under and stay in line, just the same; even the grown-up ones, like your own Ambassador, who out-ranks you by a mile. Some of them don't like it, and occasionally they strike independent attitudes; but in the end the word comes back, and the word, in one form or another, is: 'Do what the man says.'

They do what the man says, because, in this sensitive area, they cannot afford the shadow of a black mark. We always have the last word, because of that magic label 'Security'. We have the whip hand. There is no other hand worth having.

In twenty years, I can only remember one real, stand-up clash, where this whip hand was concerned. It happened near the beginning of my security career.

I had been sent to join the staff of our Embassy in Ceylon. I was 'Additional for Advisory Duties'; it was a new appointment, for an old reason—we weren't satisfied with the way the Embassy was being run, from the security angle. There had been rumours of laxity, a happy-go-lucky atmosphere which frankly had no place in the drill-book. All they told me at home, apart from showing me a few appropriate reports, was: 'If things need tightening up, say so.'

I travelled out; I joined the Embassy; I made my number with the Ambassador, a jovial, high-living character who entertained lavishly and had an enormous number of friends—perhaps too many—in Ceylon. He didn't seem to have any idea of why I was there; at the end of our interview he waved his hand cheerfully and said:

'Well, have a look around. The place is yours. But don't forget the party on Wednesday.'

I had a look around, and it did not take long for me to come up with something. The Embassy was deplorably run: in fact, it wasn't run at all—it ran itself, like some drunken office picnic. There didn't seem to be any rules. Top Secret files were passed from hand to hand, or even left on other people's desks if they were away, instead of being properly signed for, In and Out, at the central registry. Four unauthorized people knew the combination to the main safe (which held the diplomatic code-books, as well as everything else); and at least two of these men—even this wasn't very difficult to find out—had the number jotted down on the underside of their desk-calendars.

The Embassy chauffeur—a Cingalese who had been given only the most rudimentary screening—was often left in charge of the Ambassador's personal brief-case, if the latter made a duty call or attended a party on his way home. The brief-case contained any papers, in any category, which he had not had time to read during office hours.

It wasn't good enough; and after three days of careful observation, I told the Ambassador so.

At first he was incredulous—not that such things were happening, but that anyone should take them seriously.

'Good heavens, this is Ceylon!' he said, eying me as if I had taken leave of my senses. 'They haven't even *heard* about these things! Do you imagine Colombo is seething with spies? People here don't walk about picking up files off desks! They wouldn't dream of doing such a thing. Things are as safe here as if they were in a bank vault!'

'I don't think it matters whether it's Colombo or Lisbon,' I answered, as politely as I could. He was a good deal older than I; this was his fifth tour *en poste*; I just wanted to tighten things up, get the Embassy back on the rails. 'There are basic security regulations, and they've been made for a good reason.' I told him some more of the irregularities I had seen. 'I think we might be heading for trouble, if things go on like this.'

He frowned, as he had frowned during my recital of what must have sounded like a list of trivial pin-pricks. 'Lot of damn nonsense. . . . Nobody bothers about that sort of thing here. And nothing's gone wrong, has it?'

'It's difficult to check on that,' I said. His dismissive manner was beginning to grate. 'I'll have to ask you to make some changes.'

'*You'll* have to ask me?' He had quickly lost his joviality. 'Young man, I think you have an exaggerated idea of your position on my staff.'

'I've been sent here to advise you on security matters. There's a right way and a wrong way of doing these things. From what I've seen so far, a lot of people are using the wrong way.'

As men do when they know they're out of line, he elected to take this personally. 'You mean, *I'm* doing these things the wrong way?'

I wasn't ready for a collision; indeed, there didn't seem any need for one. 'Sir, security rules are being broken here. Not necessarily by you. But certainly by your staff. And you are in general charge.'

He exploded at last. 'You're damned right I'm in general charge! And I'm in particular charge, too! This is my Embassy. These people are my own staff. I trust them. We've all got along very well so far—very well indeed.' His manner made it clear that I would never be included in this cosy family. 'There's such a thing as too much enthusiasm, particularly from a new man. I suppose you people have to find something wrong, or you'd be out of a job. But you're not going to find anything wrong here.'

'I have already.'

'We'll see about that. You security experts aren't the only people in the world, you know. Even though some of you seem to think you own the place!' (This, then, was the root of the matter; he broke the rules because he didn't like the rulers.) 'Let me tell you, for a start, that this is my Embassy, and I'm going to run it my way, and no policemen are going to tell me otherwise.'

I said: 'I think they will.'

Of course, he was furious. I was waved away, into purdah, into outer space; I spent five days in leprous isolation, while all around me mouths were tightened, glances averted, and telegrams flew in all directions, demanding my head on a diplomatic pike. I only

6

cabled one report, to the right man—my boss, the man who had sent me out to sweep up the mess. Then we all waited, in a sulphurous silence.

It was, as we say, a good morning for whistling when the answer arrived. The Ambassador was recalled forthwith, for urgent consultation. He didn't come back to Ceylon, or anywhere else, and by the time the new man was appointed, that Embassy was sewn up as tight as a regimental drum. I happen to know that it has stayed that way ever since.

That was the first and last time that I ever had to argue about the rules. Perhaps the word got around. But if they still call me the Drill-Pig, that is all right with me. It means that they remember who really gives the orders.

The case of Smith and Jones (as I have chosen to call them) was my case. I was involved in it from the very beginning; firstly because their Foreign Service records were part of my particular file, secondly because I took separate chances on both of them, and lost both times. Smith and Jones, together, once cost me a promotion; now they seem to have cost me my job. Sitting it out in disgrace—the actual category is 'Suspended Duty'—while the backroom boys decide what to do with me, is a good opportunity to put the whole thing on record. I shall need it for the inquiry, anyway. For all the inquiries.

It was my case, and I knew a lot about it. You should not be surprised how much I know, how full the detail is. We know these things about almost everybody. It is not guesswork. This is the twentieth century, and when we watch people, we really watch them. The story of Smith and Jones, as I can tell it, is the product of continuous, unremitting surveillance, spying, eavesdropping, wire-tapping, hidden tape-recorders, informing, provocation, and above all minutely detailed cross-filing.

I knew what Smith and Jones were doing, nearly all the time; my coverage was just about as complete as it could possibly be. Wire-tapping is accurate and constant. Binoculars are powerful. Informers and gossip-mongers are zealous. Servants are glad of the extra money. Waiters, tuning-out the rattle of plates and cutlery, can hear the dropped voice with fantastic clarity. But mostly it is the blessings of science which bring results. Nowadays, you can listen to a conversation a mile away, simply by beaming a microphone onto the speakers—just as you might focus a telescope. (I think the other side have that one now, but we were certainly the first with it.)

You can see that we used all our toy weapons on Smith and Jones. The fact that the weapons were not enough is currently being blamed on me; and I can agree that because I didn't bear down hard all the time, because I didn't stick to the rule-book—which says that a weak man is a risk totally unacceptable, because I gave them both another chance at a crucial moment, all the rest followed naturally. Of course, they were trash, both of them, and I was perfectly aware of it. For various reasons, I didn't act on that knowledge; I wasn't consistently tough. But that will show on the record.

The record will also show that there were a lot of other people involved in this same soft attitude.

It is not my job to excuse Smith and Jones, even though I know how and why they need excusing, and can point out exactly where they were flawed. It is not my job to make allowances for weakness —if one did that, one would never stop, and the fabric of discipline would crumble to nothing. I am a Security policeman. For us, there can only be right and wrong, with no shades in between. This is a rough league, and we can't afford the luxury of shades. That is the only possible basis of operation. It is also the only possible angle from which to tell this story.

As I said, it's all set out in the rule-book, and if I had stuck to that, I wouldn't be out in the cold. But I have some company out in the cold, and I'm going to make that clear also. If you like you can write me off as a man with a grievance. But I don't intend to take the blame for a tender area of Foreign Service internal politics, where the rule-book is sometimes tucked away behind an exotic curtain of privilege. Somewhere along the line, it was indicated to me that Smith and Jones—and especially Jones—were special people for whom excuses could be made, and regulations relaxed. I fell for that; I thought it was true. I would never fall for it again.

That is something else we can't afford. Two greys

don't make a black or a white. They only make two greys.

Well, the story follows; the case-book of 'Smith and Jones'. I've changed a few other names here and there; not to protect the innocent—there are no innocents in diplomacy—but just to keep something in reserve. It will do no harm for certain people to recognize themselves under a modest disguise; I may need a pension, before very long.

Where the main story is concerned, you won't have much difficulty in guessing who I'm talking about. Everyone knows Smith and Jones.

Two

FILES are everything. You cannot run any sort of undertaking without them; and, where our security pattern is concerned, an exhaustive filing system, constantly fed and checked, is like the blood in the body. Without it, the body withers and dies, and, for all the profit it will bring you, you might as well drop the corpse into the lake.

A good memory is a good asset; but a thousand good memories cannot match the machine which embalms the facts, for all eternity, in cold clear print. Men disappear; machines live on, ever serviceable, never forgetful, nursing their own dusty grudges, recording their own bleak praise.

Files are my job. I like them very much.

At the time of Smith and Jones, I had roughly two thousand of them to take care of—that is, two thousand people, plus all the wandering tracks which led to and from them. Browsing through those files was like visiting a colossal orphanage; as if these people were my children, and I their only foster-parent.

No—that is a lot too fanciful. It was not really an orphanage at all; it had become more like a reform school. And keeping track of it, and of what the problem-children were doing, was mostly a plodding job; mental leg-work, in which you might walk a five-mile corridor of print to turn up a single fact.

The occasional drama—like the Smith and Jones affair—was due to one thing only; when you turned up the fact, it didn't register properly.

Both Smith and Jones had nice thick files. It was not a measure of their rank, since they were both in comparatively minor jobs; it meant that their official lives had had their ups and downs, mostly for per-sonal reasons. A career Ambassador who never put a foot wrong had an average file; an Agricultural Attaché who took to the bottle or the wrong bed was worth his weight in paper.

Smith was a good example of a man substantially outweighed by his own record. If we take a look at his file—which I certainly know well enough—I can fill in the details as we go along.

At the time of which I speak, Ivan Percival Smith was 46; married for eight years; no children; serving (after seventeen years in the Foreign Service) in the grade of First Secretary, which was a notch or two below what he should have reached if his career had gone smoothly. As a young man he had given himself a sort of spare-time classical education, rare in this country. He was a language expert (French, German, Spanish, Arabic). He had served in London, Madrid, Paris, Buenos Aires and Cairo. He had been seconded for advisory duties with our military mission to Korea in 1952, and again (in the role of what we called Special Assistant) to Turkey in 1958. His hobbies were listed as 'Reading, Music, Dining out.'

The final notation in his private file read: 'Not above Minister-Counsellor.' Frankly, knowing him as I knew him, it was easy to see why.

To begin with, Smith's appearance was against him. He was a big fat man, sloppily dressed, massively unco-ordinated; when he walked towards you along a corridor it was like a sluggish tide swirling up a narrow channel of rock. He was slow, and easy-going, and he made something of a cult of this. He had a liking for Latin tags, and his favourite was: 'Suaviter in modo.' He was always using it; at office conferences, at parties in night-clubs, at times of crisis or confusion.

'Suaviter in modo,' he would say, in rebuke of a colleague too zealous or too excitable in committee. 'Suaviter in modo,' he would intone, in his rich fruity voice, when he had had too much to drink and had to negotiate from a restaurant dining-room to the street outside. 'Suaviter in modo,' he would mutter, as he stumbled head-first into a taxi.

I never had a classical education, and I had to look it up, the first time I heard it. '*Suaviter in modo*' means 'gentle in manner' or, as ordinary people would say, 'Take it easy.' It is half of a phrase which goes '*Suaviter in modo, fortiter in re,*' meaning 'Gentle in manner, strong in action.' Once, when Smith was having one of the habitual rows with his wife in the Milroy Club in London, he used the whole quotation, and his wife snapped back: 'Well, you're good for half of that. I'll give evidence, any time.'

That brings us to the wife, another—and crucial—smudge on the career of Ivan Percival Smith. She was English, and rich, and dissatisfied; we did not encourage any of these deviations. A foreign-born wife (even from so well-balanced a country as England) posed certain problems; she would have friends who perhaps should not be her husband's friends; she would have prejudices which he should not share, and should not be exposed to. She was a kind of hostage, a neutral just where neutrality mattered most.

A rich wife could be an asset, but only up to a certain point. If she spent her money on entertaining, all very well; if she used it to give her husband independence, a sense of freedom from the ultimate pressure of authority, then she was not doing him any good. We did not pay our diplomats to be free agents. We paid them to toe the line—our line.

Above all, a dissatisfied wife was a particular brand of nuisance. Diplomatic wives were dissatisfied for two reasons, either professional or sexual; in both areas (as I once heard a Frenchman phrase it) she felt he was not rising high enough. In the case of Ivan Percival Smith, we suspected that the trouble was marital, within the narrow meaning of the word. He wasn't delivering what she had really paid for.

Perhaps the clue was that 'no children' entry on his file, coupled with the late marriage (marriage at 38 was always a questionable conversion—i.e., conversion from what?). Perhaps it was Mrs. Smith's broad hints to an indiscreet number of friends, or her recurrent love-affairs with those minor Latin diplomats who, in all other respects, must be seriously under-employed. Perhaps it was Smith himself—his sensuous tastes, his heavy, almost avuncular manner towards his colleagues and his friends, his preference for all-male dinner parties. At any rate, we had a query against him in that particular column, and were ready for the evidence.

The last doubt which stemmed from the bare facts of the file was Korea. Owing to some mix-up over truce-lines and safe-conducts, Smith had been taken prisoner in Korea. We were able to arrange an exchange for him, but not before he had spent eight months in captivity. When he returned, he had very little to say, except that he had been fairly treated. We didn't like that at all. Brain-washing showed itself in various forms. One of them was this negative attitude.

So much for Smith, a man of taste, talent, and independence, not to be promoted above Minister-

Counsellor. Jones was a different animal altogether, at least on the surface.

He was much younger, only 27, at the beginning of a career as Cultural Attaché which had already brought him, and us, a load of trouble. He had a long list of black marks—brawls in bars, speeding offences, scenes at parties, public insults—which should really have got him dismissed already. The fact that they had not done so is something I shall be coming back to. When a man attracts so much unfavourable notice, and manages, time and again, to get away with it, he probably has an exceptional kind of pull.

Peter Paul Jones, aged 27; unmarried; employed as Cultural Attaché successively in London, Leopold-ville, Cairo, Rio de Janeiro, Belgrade, and Tel Aviv (he had twice served at the same embassies as Smith). Average length of tour: six months. Average reason for being moved on: a small or a large scandal.

I had met Jones on a number of occasions, and liked him less each time. He was a small, very elegant young man; quick-witted, a great gossip, a great party-goer, a swift and sly drinker. The silk suits from Rome, the ruffled cream shirts from New York, the batiste ties from Charvet of Paris, all bespoke a certain kind of decadent taste; the curly blond hair and slight willowy figure told the rest of the story. To survive in the Foreign Service—even to be employed there in the first place—he must have had special friends in special places, all of the same persuasion.

Like nearly all other governments, our position on

homosexuals was one of extreme caution. It was not prejudice so much as hard experience. We had learned, over many years, that however gifted they might be, the chance was scarcely worth taking. They attracted trouble; they made trouble; they were exceptionally liable to cause public scandal, to drown their sorrows and shortcomings in alcohol, to make friends and lose them in the most damaging circumstances. The special relationship, chancy and inconclusive, seemed to make for violent quarrels and jealousies, usually resolved at the top of the voice at diplomatic receptions. Perhaps the uproar was necessary, taking the place of a more fulfilling act of love. At any rate, it always happened.

Finally, they invited the kind of blackmail which must inevitably destroy their usefulness. A man afraid of this particular exposure would do anything to escape it. He would sell himself. He would sell his country. He would sell anything entrusted to him.

Jones—a junior grade expert on documentary films, art exhibitions, books, and such-like—had never been entrusted with much, and, if I had anything to do with it, he never would be. He was a nuisance rather than a danger; but even so, I would have got rid of him long ago. He had left behind him, even in a short career, a whole train of mischief. Mostly it was his tongue which got him into trouble; he would go to parties, get moderately drunk, and either quarrel with a fellow guest, or start to cry, or come out with eminently quotable insults about other members of the Diplomatic Corps, or prominent figures in the host country, or local customs, or touchy areas of national pride.

He seemed fated to say the wrong thing, and to enjoy the resulting commotion. To him, as to many others, a vicious row was irresistible, bitterness was sweet.

In spite of obvious differences, it was probable that Smith and Jones were two of a kind. They were known to be friends; indeed, there was a record on the file of a joint indiscretion which, though it had nothing to do with this particular problem, should have warned us of a kind of unwholesome communion.

It had happened in Cairo, at a reception for one of those scruffy little African 'new nations' whom everyone flatters and no one believes in—except as a voter at U.N. For some reason, Smith on the night in question was in a mood of austerity; he had been holding forth for some time about the iniquity of expensive diplomatic entertaining in a starving world. Given the lavishness of President Nasser's hospitality, the topic was unfortunate. Jones, who was also in the group, and drunk, was even more explicit.

'It's really too monstrous!' he declared loudly, hitching his shoulders for further emphasis. 'What are we doing, swilling down champagne when most of the world is destitute?' He waved away a huge tray of caviar and smoked salmon *canapés*, as if they were poisoned. 'How can we justify truckloads of stuff like that going to waste, when even the people we represent are short of food?'

A Yugoslav in the circle picked this up very sharply. 'You mean,' he commented slyly, 'your own people are starving?'

There was an awkward pause. Then Smith, who had actually sparked the conversation, said: 'No. Of course not.'

But Jones said: 'Yes. Some of them.'

The exchange reached the newspapers, as, in a whispering-gallery like Cairo, it was bound to. There was a minor scandal, and a soothing press release. Smith was reprimanded. Jones, not for the first time, was moved on.

As I said, Smith and Jones were two of a kind; but the fact wasn't noted, or given its proper weight, until it was too late. Or, if it was noted, someone with the right kind of eraser rubbed it out again, blew on the page, destroyed all the evidence, and kept on doing so.

It must have happened with both of them. Smith with the troublesome wife and the exotic tastes, Jones the persistent public trouble-maker—no one ever did anything about them. There was a concerted hands-off policy. They both seemed to have more friends in high places than any man who might try to throw them out. Round them was a subtle aura of accommodation, as if for privileged people.

I even caught a whiff of it myself, on one important occasion.

It concerned something which had happened in Belgrade, to Jones, and this time he was in big trouble. He had been caught for speeding and drunk driving before. But this time he had killed someone, and the heat was really on.

I was present, officially, when Jones was hauled up before our Ambassador. Jones would have to leave Belgrade immediately—that much was certain, and within the limits of his diplomatic immunity. But there was also a question whether he should leave the Foreign Service as well. I was there to give an opinion, from our own angle.

I watched him carefully as he stood on the carpet in front of the Ambassador's desk. He was much the worse for wear; apart from the hangover, which was obvious, he had spent the night in jail, in spite of our best efforts to have him released. The silk suit was rumpled and stained, the handsome face grey with worry and fatigue.

For the second time, the Ambassador—a small, fussy, and also badly worried man—put his question.

'But why did you do it? You must have known you were quite unfit to drive! Yet you rush out of a party like a damned lunatic, and drive off without lights! Why did you *do* it?'

Jones, who had not answered before, now raised his head. He looked completely washed out; the shadows under his eyes were black smudges; the lips were pinched and quivering. He said, in a low voice:

'I was in despair.'

The phrase, which I found theatrical and absurd, hung in the air between us all. It was an embarrassing moment. Then Jones suddenly cried out: 'I'm sorry! Oh God, I'm sorry!' and burst into tears.

The Ambassador, taken aback, said: 'We'll have to find somewhere where you can't make any more trouble.'

'Anywhere!' gulped Jones, sobbing.

When he had been dismissed, in a state of collapse which I thought rather overdone, the Ambassador looked across at me. 'Well? What do you think?'

'He'll have to leave Belgrade tonight,' I answered. 'It needs to be cleared with the Justice Department, and with Protocol. They'll simply declare him *persona non grata*. There'll be a row in the press, of course, but if he's not here it will die away. We'd better say that he's been sacked.' I glanced at him. 'I imagine that will be true, anyway.'

The Ambassador, more composed and more careful, said: 'I'm not too sure about that. . . . Everyone makes mistakes. . . . He's been under great strain, I happen to know. . . . We'll have to think carefully before sending the report.'

He talked a lot more in this sense; I became aware of what I had heard rumoured before—that there was a special climate of protection, special dispensation, for this favoured young man. He had friends, relatives, connections, leads to this official and to that. Gradually it became clear that Jones, after doing suitable penance, would be employed again, and that no good would be served by advising other-wise.

I resented the fact; it was the sort of thing which would never happen to me. But it wasn't important enough to merit the risk of defeat. For somewhere along the line, during the next twenty-four hours, it was hinted that this might be a very good tide for me to swim with; perhaps the only tide; perhaps the only way to swim. Finally, reluctantly, I went on record as saying: 'Give him another chance.' It was a mistake, and I wouldn't repeat it today. But I did say it then.

Jones was sent home. Then he was reappointed, to Tel Aviv, and I heard nothing of him until he was hauled up, once again, this time for making a drunk-en, maudlin speech about the forgiveness of sins, and finally proposing a two minutes' silence for Colonel Eichmann.

Apparently I had made a mistake over Jones, and I heard about that also, from superiors who did not have to swim with any stream thus muddied. Just before it came out, however, I made one more. This time it was Smith.

Three

THIS time it was Smith; it must have been his turn for trouble. Smith and his wife—her name was Patricia—were on their way to take up his latest posting, which was to that part of the world which, as far as we were concerned, had now settled into permanent enmity. They stopped over in London, with official permission, and after checking in at our own Embassy they had a week's free time.

They used it as they might have been expected to do. Patricia Smith saw her family, and a lot of old friends, and spent a small fortune on clothes, including a £3,000 chinchilla coat which she excused carelessly as being essential for 'that hideous climate.' Ivan Smith dived heavily and happily into the pleasures of the table. In fact, during their week's leave they saw very little of each other. But they gave a party together on their last night in London; a

dinner-party for eight at one of their favourite restaurants—the White Tower in Soho; and at that
party they had a final, knock-down-and-drag-out
row, and Patricia Smith walked out on him for ever.

We received very full accounts of that row—not
that we had anyone at the White Tower; but the
restaurant is popular with diplomats, and one of
them was good enough to report and confirm a scene
which was hardly kept private in any case. From this,
and from a talkative friend who was actually one of
the Smiths' guests at dinner, I was able to construct a
complete picture of a disgraceful occasion.

Apparently it was clear to the other guests, from
the outset, that both their host and hostess were in a
bad temper, and would rather have spent this last
evening apart. Smith, fond of male company and
having another weakness also—poker—had had to
turn down an invitation to a final poker-party with
some particular cronies, and was in a mood of glum
resignation. Mrs. Smith had spent the day with her
mother, who lived in considerable splendour in Belgrave Square, and was known to have a poor opinion
of her son-in-law's capabilities, prospects, and general
treatment of her darling daughter. She had probably
made Patricia Smith, if not homesick for life in
England, at least discontented with the prospect of
another three or four years' exile.

There was something else equally clear to all the
guests as they assembled at the White Tower; that the
Smiths had both had plenty to drink already.

According to report, gourmets thought a lot of the White Tower; its speciality was Greek dishes. The guests ordered their food with care; but when it came to Smith's turn, he remained slumped in his chair at the top of the table, waved the head-waiter and the menu away, and said loudly:

'Oh God, I don't care! Bring me anything. Bring me some soup.'

'And to follow, sir?'

'I'll think about it. Don't bother me now.'

His voice and his manner were both conspicuous. All the guests affected not to notice either; not so Mrs. Smith. She also raised her voice, from the other end of the table:

'You'd better eat,' she called out. 'It's the last good meal you'll get for three years.'

It was a silly thing to say; it would have been silly to say it even in private. A lot of people within earshot knew where the Smiths were going; such remarks have a tendency to travel ahead, and to greet one on arrival, sometimes at a press conference. Smith, conscious of a public *gaffe*, frowned at his wife and said:

'I didn't know the English were such experts. . . . The food will be perfectly adequate.'

Mrs. Smith gave him a cold and calculated stare. 'The English were enjoying civilized cooking,' she said with crisp contempt, 'when you people were eating raw meat with your fingers.'

After a pause, everyone at the table started talking at once, on a somewhat determined note; there was a positive outburst of social camouflage. Smith and his wife glared at each other, but for the moment they had been separated. The meal proceeded normally for some time, though it could hardly be said to be a social triumph. Then came the explosion which finished it, and a lot of other things as well.

Smith was eating nothing; it became obvious that he was only going to drink, in sulky isolation, for the rest of that evening. There came a moment when he wanted to order another bottle of wine; and in gesturing for the wine-waiter's attention, he knocked over the ice-bucket at his elbow, with a resounding crash. It produced instant silence, and in that silence Mrs. Smith spoke again:

'My dear husband,' she said, 'is edgy tonight. To say the least.'

The man sitting on her right, a Brazilian diplomat with faultless party manners, sought to smooth over what looked like another approaching storm.

'He should rather be happy,' he declared reassuringly. 'It is a very good appointment.'

'It's a rotten appointment,' said Mrs. Smith, loudly and clearly. 'As usual . . . And what about me?'

'I confess I do not understand,' said the Brazilian, aware of failure already.

'What about me?' repeated Mrs. Smith. The other guests had abandoned all pretence of not listening, and there was now complete silence round the table. 'God, do you think I want to live in that damned place, without a soul to talk to? I might as well be buried alive! In an ice-box! They don't even know how to dress properly!'

At the other end of the table, Smith roused himself at last. He probably realized that it would have been better to pass the thing off somehow, but his bitter mood would not allow it.

'That'll do, Patricia,' he said, with a very unlikely display of authority. 'We're going there, and that's all there is to it. It's my job.'

'It's my job!' she mimicked, suddenly furious again. 'Heavens, do I have to listen to that feeble alibi *every* day? You'd say "It's my job" if they handed you a mop and told you to clean out the chancery! If you were half a man, you'd get yourself a better one.' She gave him a long stare. 'If you were half a man, you'd do a lot of other things better, too.'

One of the women guests giggled: the allusion had been made disgustingly clear. Smith, belatedly aware of an appalling situation, backed away from it. 'Take it easy,' he muttered. '*Suaviter in modo.*'

'Don't say that!' Suddenly Mrs. Smith's voice was a strident scream. 'If you say that again, I'll brain you! We've had eight solid years of *suavitor in modo*, and look where it's got you.' She stood up, knocking over her chair; she was absolutely, uncontrollably furious. 'Well, it hasn't got *me* there! You want to go and live in that barbarian dump? Go ahead! I'm staying where I am, here in London.'

'Patricia!' Smith had half risen from his place. 'You can't behave like this!'

'Just watch me!' She gave him a last murderous look; it seemed to hold eight years of disillusion, eight years' crude contempt. 'Oh, you needn't get the vapours again. I'll pay the bill here.'

She then turned and marched out of the restaurant, chinchilla coat and all, leaving the ruins of her dinner party in shattered silence, and a husband who looked, appropriately, as if he had been hit on the head with a full bottle.

Smith had indeed been hit very hard, but he recovered swiftly, at least on the surface; it was for him a point of pride to believe that no woman could damage him. He was in touch with our Embassy very early next morning; on the telephone, and later in the office, he was entirely frank with authority. He had had a monumental row with his wife, the last of many; she had left him, and was holed up in her mother's house in Belgrave Square; she wouldn't come out, and Smith couldn't get in.

He was due to leave England by an evening flight, in less than twelve hours, to take up his new posting. What should he do?

It was a surprise, but an Ambassador has many surprises; our man in London remained professionally calm. After a short consultation, Smith was told to postpone leaving London for forty-eight hours, while the facts were referred home, and we thought them over.

It was not an easy choice; when the file landed on

my desk, I weighed the pros and cons for a long time. Smith of course had been announced as a married man, both in the press and as regards his accreditation; accommodation had been arranged for him on that basis; if he turned up without his wife, how was it to be explained? Suppose Mrs. Smith sued for divorce, or for a legal separation, what would the publicity—there might be a lot—do to his position? Would it be better if he were re-posted to a more anonymous job at home, till the thing was resolved, one way or the other?

Above all, what would the separation do to *him*, and to his work? Would he miss his wife, and mope? Would he *not* miss her, and behave like a bachelor? Would he go sour, or settle down, or burst out?

It was the last point I talked about, when I took the problem to my head-of-section. He would be sending the new orders, whatever they were; but I had to give the advice, and it had to be good.

'I don't believe the quarrel will make a lot of difference to him,' I said, when I had presented my outline. I had been making up my mind to this end for the past hour; it might have been a self-delusion, to save us trouble, but I don't think that was a factor. 'In fact, Smith could be better off without her. They were always having rows. Now he can relax and get down to his work.'

My section-head—whose name was Colonel Bellinger—was as usual staring at me fixedly while I spoke. This was a habitual trick of his, and perhaps a good one; it made you think either that what you were saying was sounding sillier by the moment, or that you had something dirty on your face. It put you in the wrong, which was where a subordinate ought to be. Colonel Bellinger was a small prim man with a small prim mouth, and this was another familiar pattern; a lot of my superiors seemed to be cast in the same mould; one day, I would probably achieve it myself—the cultivated primness, anyway. It was of course entirely false. We could not be shocked, either professionally or personally; but to look as if we could was liable to put the other man, once again, in the wrong. Nor was anybody particularly prim when it came to discipline, in or outside the Security Branch. In that area, wax faces melted and the hard fist took over.

Now Colonel Bellinger said: 'But they are married.' This was a good example of fake prudery. Bellinger thought as much of the sanctity of marriage as he did of the sanctity of human life; in case of need, they were both as expendable as a rusty nail. What he was saying, of course, was a shorthand version of a public attitude. Smith was a married man; his wife should be by his side, faithful, industrious, and true. Anything else was probably sin.

'She was never any use to him,' I countered. 'And if she hates the country, and doesn't mind saying so—because of all that money—' (this was my own brand of shorthand) '—then she could do him, and us, a lot of harm.'

'What will he do, living by himself?' asked Colonel Bellinger.

It was vaguely phrased, but we both knew what this one was about. I had been giving it a lot of thought, and now I came out with the result.

'I think that'll be all right,' I said. 'He doesn't seem to be the active kind. Sort of neuter. I think he'll settle down by himself.'

That seemed to be enough for Colonel Bellinger, and it seemed to suit him also; the questionable topic had been primly disposed of. There remained one more, and he now brought it up.

'If he goes out there alone, what do we say?'

I had worked that one out, too. 'She hasn't been too well,' I answered. 'She's staying on in England for reasons of health.' I smiled, allowing myself a minor joke. 'However unlikely that may seem.' The joke lapped against Colonel Bellinger's tight mouth, discovered no opening, and fell back into the sea. 'Or that she wants to spend more time with her mother, who isn't well either. Both of those will do all right.'

'Unless she starts talking,' said Colonel Bellinger. 'She might say something quite different, just to annoy him. And us. That had better be cleared in London. Get them to find out if she'll go along with a health story, and promise to stick to it.'

'Yes, sir.'

Colonel Bellinger had been maintaining his fixed stare; now he dropped his eyes momentarily, as if shielding a new thought which was not quite ready for the fresh air. Presently he said:

'I suppose we couldn't persuade her to go.'

The word 'persuade' was so delicately mouthed that I knew it was another of his shorthand twirls. I answered it in the same way.

'No. That's out of the question. Her mother has too many friends.'

It was a fact that we could not make her go with her husband. Mrs. Smith had never become a citizen —which was another point against Smith; if we put on any sort of pressure, there could be a tremendous scandal. And force—

'Force is out of the question,' said Colonel Bellinger suddenly. 'Anyway, we don't do that sort of thing. *They* do it.'

I let that argument lie where it was, without comment. Instead, I went back to the main issue.

'I think he should go by himself,' I said. 'Changing plans at the last moment would cause more talk than it's worth.' There was an additional point, which I had not brought up; that Smith should not be allowed to get out of his appointment, for this or any other reason. His posting was not exactly a medal pinned on his chest; it was a chore, to be dutifully undertaken in a country where, as Mrs. Smith had said, there wasn't a soul to talk to, and the climate was awful. Our presence there was only a diplomatic token; we would not make any friends, in a hundred years, because we didn't intend to. But we all had to take our turn at the polite charade. This was Smith's turn.

'Very well,' said Colonel Bellinger. His finger-tips came precisely together; it was his sign-off for the interview. 'He can go, if she will keep quiet. But that must be cleared first. Perhaps a written undertaking. The English believe in them. . . . We don't want any sudden long-range quarrelling.'

Mrs. Smith said that she would keep quiet; indeed, as she told a startled Second Secretary at our London Embassy, she never wanted to hear the bastard's name again. We took her word for that, and Smith went off, two days late. Pretty soon I began to forget about him; he seemed to be keeping clear of trouble, and there were a lot of more important worries about that time.

Even when, a little later on, someone in the office said (I think quite innocently): 'Oh well, Smith won't be too lonely. He'll have one friend there. Jones is going out'—even then, I did not think twice about it. There was a gentle tug at the memory; no more. But it was a fact that they were moving towards their appointment, and I had sent them to it.

Four

THE awakening, about a year later, was rough; the roughest of my career. It came in the form of an inter-office telephone call, from another part of the Security building. It was Colonel Bellinger, and his tone was formidable.

'We've just lost two diplomats,' he said curtly, without preamble, 'Your Mr. Smith and your Mr. Jones.'

I was taken aback; too much so to sort out the implication of the word 'your', though it registered strongly enough. 'Lost? I don't understand.'

'*I* don't understand,' said Bellinger, in the same tone. 'But I will. . . . Smith and Jones have disappeared, and our Embassy doesn't know where they are.'

'When was this?' I asked, trying to get something to go on while I was thinking it out.

'No details yet,' answered Colonel Bellinger. I could almost feel him staring at me, reacting to a stupid question. 'Just the bare report. They're not in their offices; they're not at home, they're not on leave, and they haven't been in touch since the day before yesterday.'

'There could have been an accident.'

'It would have been reported by now.'

'Or they're out on some sort of a party.'

'Not for forty-eight hours. Or if they are, it's the last party they'll go to.' There was a pause; he was obviously very angry; I could think of nothing else to say. Then his voice barked out: '*Well?*'

'Sir, I don't know. I suppose we'll have to wait.'

'Till we read about it in the newspapers? Is that the i

⎿t may be nothing.'

'And it may be a hell of a lot!' His voice slowed down, to a grim warning recital. 'Look, don't let's fool with this. I've a damned good idea of what's happened, and if what I suspect is true, you'd better get ready to start looking for your friends.'

The receiver clicked. He had said his piece, and made his point again. I didn't like the sound of it at all. It turned out to be the first of a long list of things I didn't like, both on that day and on many days afterwards.

The story reached the newspapers that same evening; one of their friends, or someone at the Embassy, must have talked. The item itself was handled non-committally; obviously the papers were not going to make too much of it until there were more pointers. Smith and Jones were 'missing'; their whereabouts was a 'mystery'; their friends were baffled, and the police were making urgent inquiries to uncover the reason for their disappearance.

It was a guarded story, into which one might read anything one chose. But it had a small, lethal sting in its tail. It mentioned that Smith had once been a prisoner in Korea, that Jones was well known as an enthusiastic party-goer, and that the two were 'firm friends'. The three clues, neatly dropped, were enough to steer speculation up a definite alley. The public, adding up a few sums, was certainly ready for the real news, when it broke.

It broke at noon next day. Up till then, all we had to go on, officially, was a statement that the police were still searching for missing diplomats Smith and Jones. This was not true. It turned out that the police had them already, in the warmest embrace this side of suffocation.

It came as a midday news-flash on the radio. It was only half a dozen sentences, but it was enough to start the avalanche. The missing diplomats, Smith and Jones, had asked for political asylum. In a joint statement, they had declared: 'We wish to live in a free society, where there is no war-psychosis, no bureaucratic tyranny, and an opportunity for all.' They had been granted temporary refuge while their application was considered. Meanwhile, at their own request, they were *incommunicado*.

The phone jangled even as I was listening to the broadcast. It was not Colonel Bellinger himself. It was a message from him, relayed by an aide with crisp relish. I was to report to the Colonel's office now, immediately.

Bellinger was on the telephone when I got to his office, and he was listening, not talking; the steady sharp crackle on the line, and his stony face, told a whole story in themselves. Finally he said: 'Yes, Mr. Secretary—I'll take care of that,' and put the receiver down, very slowly, very deliberately.

'You can guess who that was,' he said. His voice was tight and thin; he had been angry when he first gave me the news, now he was coldly furious. 'Bawling *me* out. . . . *Me!* . . . Well, now it's my turn. . . . You heard what happened?'

'Yes, sir.'

'And?'

It was a time to be wary, very wary. 'It's not exactly a thing you can foresee.'

'Is that your only comment?'

I couldn't fight back until I knew what there was to fight. 'Sir, there've been people before who—'

'You damned fool!' he burst out suddenly. It was not a loud shout, but it penetrated like a switch-knife, darting, snake-like. 'Of course there have been people before! That's why we have a Security Branch. To see that it doesn't happen again. That's what we're here for. That's why you're employed here, so that I can ask you questions, and you can give me the right answers. And now it *has* happened again, to us. You know why?'

I could see it coming; I couldn't ward it off; whatever I said, the result was going to be the same. Bellinger, using an emergency net, had snared me for the leading role. In those circumstances, I wasn't going to beg.

'We made a mistake,' I said, as matter-of-factly as I could. 'You just can't guarantee that people won't go off the rails. Smith and Jones—'

'Smith and Jones are a couple of first-class security risks, and you should have worked that out long ago. You had all the facts in your files, and yet you gave me the wrong answers.' He was staring at me in enraged hatred. 'And don't try that "we" stuff, because I'm not going to buy it. I know exactly what you said about each of them; it's down here on the record, in black and white.' He tapped a sheet of paper in front of him; he must have ordered it made out, ready for this very interview, as soon as the first news broke. 'You told me that it was safe for Smith to take up his appointment. That the quarrel with his wife didn't matter. That he was probably better off without her. And about Jones—' his glance flickered down to the paper, then up again, '—you specifically told our Ambassador in Belgrade that Jones should be given another chance. The day after he'd killed somebody! He would have been sacked, otherwise—

sacked! All this time, you've been sitting on these facts, you let the two of them go off to the same Embassy—'

'Sir, that's not fair, and not accurate.' There was a very cold wind blowing round me; it might have been best to bow to it; but I couldn't take this slanted version. 'I had nothing to do with their appointments. It's true that I cleared them from the security angle, on the best available evidence. I wasn't too happy about Jones, but—'

'That's all I want to hear from you,' he broke in. His voice had altered subtly. It was as if I had dealt him exactly the right card, the fifth of a straight flush; with a pat hand, he could afford to lose the edge of excitement, and sit there coolly, and wait for me to go bankrupt. 'You cleared them, and I took your word for it. In fact, you steered me completely wrong. You know what's going to happen now?'

I waited.

'You're going to untangle this one,' he went on, after a moment. 'It's *your* snarl, and you're going to unsnarl it, strand by strand, if it takes you the rest of your life. Or the rest of your time in the service.'

'Sir, I'll do what I can. But—'

'You're damned right you'll do what you can.' For the first time, the thin lips were not in a straight line; but the result was not a smile, it was a sneer. 'This office is going to be on the griddle about this. For a long time. You know what they'll be saying about our security, from now on? Well, it's not *our* security, it's *your* security, and you're going to put it right again. Otherwise, you'll be in the same boat with those two bastards, as far as we're concerned. And I mean just that.' The next sentence was a snapped order. 'As of now, you're assigned to Smith and Jones.'

'I don't see what I—'

'Jones isn't important,' Colonel Bellinger went on, as if I had not spoken. 'He's cultural. A cultural drunk. Films and pictures and books and booze. He knows nothing worthwhile. People like him are two a penny, and the price is just about right. . . . Smith *is* important. . . . He can talk a good deal, if he cares to. . . . And together, they're a propaganda gift, *your* gift. But you're going to get your gift returned. Or cancelled out. Or covered up. Somehow. Whatever happens, Smith and Jones aren't going to matter in the future. You're going to put the clock back again.'

He paused. The order had been issued. There wasn't going to be any argument. I felt as if I had been pushed out, alone, to the end of a long branch, and told never to come back the same way; to stay there, in fact, until I had learned to fly. I was being given a rotten job, probably an impossible one; if Smith and Jones had defected, how could they be lured back? Men did not take this giant step save as a desperate act of flight, hacking down all bridges, burning all boats. . . . *And it was not my fault.* . . . But these were private thoughts, for sorting out later. Now was the time for a good face.

'I'll do my best, sir,' I said.

'It had better be good enough.' He was not going to give me an inch of grace. I was outside the club already; if I was to get back in, it would only be by earning it, by showing results. He made that very clear when he added: 'I don't want any negative reports.'

'Have I got a free hand, sir?'

'You have a free hand to succeed,' His mouth was now a mean slit. 'You are to fly out there now, to-night. Your posting to the Embassy will follow. Find out all you can. Talk to the Ambassador; he's been knocked sideways by this—as well he might. Get to see Smith and Jones; they can't very well refuse that. Try to talk them out of this thing. Threaten them. Bribe them. Promote them. Find out what they want and give it to them. If that doesn't work—' his little eyes flicked sideways, '—start to discredit them. They think they're an asset? Nonsense! They're just a couple of worthless, scruffy turncoats who were due to be sacked anyway. For incompetence. For pilfering. For immorality. Something like that.' His fingertips were coming together; he was not giving this any more of his valuable time. 'That's all,' he said. And then, as an afterthought: 'We won't be able to make a vacancy in your present grade. You'll be attached as Third Secretary.'

As far as London, where I had to change planes, my thoughts were mostly personal. It was a night plane, but I could not sleep; I sat bolt upright in the narrow middle seat of a tier of three, in an aircraft which seemed to grow more uncomfortable and crowded with every mile we flew. Third Secretaries, I found, did not exactly overwork our Travel Section; they were shoved into the first available seat on the first available flight. I was booked economy class in an old Constellation, belonging to an almost nameless airline which catered chiefly to sight-seeing charter parties. No doubt it kept its eye on the pilgrim trade also.

That demotion, that elbow-grinding discomfort, was the spark for most of my thoughts.

Though I could admire how neatly I had been slipped into the villain's slot, it remained a crude trick. Colonel Bellinger, feeling the cold draught around his own head, had promptly slammed all the windows, leaving me outside. It was true that I had 'cleared' Smith and Jones, to the extent of saying that they were harmless; but Bellinger, with the same information available, had agreed with me. The way in which he had slid out of that agreement, and put the whole blame on me, would repay study. But in the meantime, I was outside in the cold, and it was going to take me a long time to get back.

He had said: 'You'll be in the same boat with those two bastards,' and I could be sure that, if I failed, he would keep his word, and pour on the necessary poison. In plain language, it meant that if I did not get Smith and Jones back again, I would be coupled with them, as a sort of contributory traitor, a third runaway. It would be the end of me, inside the Foreign Service or out of it.

It was unjust. It was brutal. But it remained a fact, and I could not see my way past it.

If it was true that Smith and Jones had defected, the chance of getting them back was remote. As well as being a giant step, it was also an irrevocable one, for all sorts of reasons. A man who took it turned an insulting back on his friends and his country; he was flattered and rewarded to the very limit by his new hosts; to retrace the step needed a double ration of guts, which a traitor rarely had. One disreputable flight was enough having; made it, he must stay where he was.

Bellinger's idea, expressed as 'Find out what they want, and give it to them', was supported by one single clue; the phrase in their fatuous proclamation about 'an opportunity for all'. Perhaps they hadn't said it—the wording of the whole thing had a propaganda ring to it—but if it reflected what they were looking for, it still wasn't much use to us. They wanted a better job, or more money, or quicker promotion; if we promised them the whole earth tomorrow, they must know that we would take it away again as soon as they were safely at home. After their flight—even if it had been impulsive, or drunken, or made under duress—we could never use them again. The stamp was on them. We could lock them up as traitors, or pension them off as amiable lunatics. But that would be the limit of their reward.

Bellinger's other idea, that if they were really lost to us, they should be discredited, was even less promising; it would convey nothing but the taste of sour grapes. Moreover, it was dangerous; it could snap back, and kick us in the teeth. It would prompt the immediate question, particularly at home: 'If they were so worthless, why were they kept on?' There was no answer to that, except to claim that they had suddenly gone bad; and it would take a lot of evidence, manufactured or not, to make that convincing. We would still look like a bunch of fools, either way.

The plane lurched in an upward current of air; the man next to me on the aisle side, a bearded Eastern Orthodox priest who looked like Makarios and whose rusty robes smelt of food and sweat, grunted in his sleep and lolled against me. I pushed him off roughly, and he opened his large brown eyes and looked at me as if I had ordered him flogged. I wished that I could do so. My thoughts had grown savage, and private. Basically, I didn't give a damn about Smith and Jones. I had my own troubles, and they were pressing down hard. I spent the rest of the long flight thinking out some way—any way—of pulling myself out of the mud.

Smith and Jones returned in full force at London, where it was raining, and I only had time to stock up with newspapers before catching my onward flight. The world's press was humming; the Smith and

Jones story, which recalled other defections on both sides of the curtain, was being played as a farce, with overtones of private corruption and public futility. The Security Branch took most of the limelight.

Why did we employ such men?—that was the gist of half the newspaper comment; the other half asked, in honest wonder, how sensitive intellectuals such as Smith and Jones had stood it so long. . . . The papers had got hold of most of the career facts, and a lot of diplomatic gossip, and were playing them for all they were worth. Where Smith was concerned, they made a big thing out of the Korean captivity, of which he was reported to have said: 'I have no complaints at all about being there.' (This was not quite true; what he had actually said was that he had no complaints about his treatment as a prisoner, which was not the same thing at all.) They had also tracked down Mrs. Smith, 'separated from her husband for personal reasons,' and she had given her own austere verdict: 'I have not seen my husband for over a year. I would not be surprised at anything he might do.'

This was headlined, naturally, as: 'WIFE NOT SURPRISED.'

Jones of course was a gift. He was given the full treatment; the parties, the public quarrels, the drunk driving, the manslaughter in Belgrade, the 'exotic circle of men friends'—all was cooked up into a savoury mixed grill of innuendo, spiced with misconduct, irrationality, and perversion. It was topped off by an exceptionally quotable quote from his

45

mother, who was reported to have confided to a close friend: 'Peter was always rather a queer little boy.' That one had gone round the world with the speed of sound.

Surrounded by newspapers, I dozed off, and awoke to read yet another paragraph about the 'official ineptitude' which had kept these men in employment long after they had shown themselves unfitted for it. I had a drink, and picked at a lavish meal (this was a much better plane, a modern jet, with three pretty girls to look after a handful of passengers), and slept again, fed up with the whole thing and no nearer a solution. I awoke to a brilliant dawn, with the sun looking at us over a distant spine of mountains, and the plane dropping down into a snowy white world, featureless, frozen in enmity.

Then I was there, in hostile territory, with a tough job to do, and nothing that I could recognize as a weapon to do it with.

Five

AMBASSADOR BLACK was a very worried man, which he had a right to be; and he was showing it, which he should not. It must have been obvious that our Embassy, and everyone in it, was now right under the spotlight, just as much as Smith and Jones. It was certainly clear enough to me, when I arrived at the squat square building which housed our mission.

Curious crowds had gathered outside, stamping their feet in the frozen slush as they waited. There was no passer-by who did not pause to look up at the empty façade, or to ask a question of the onlookers. A man in a fur-lined trench coat, note-book at the ready, had tried to interview me as I went up the front steps, and when I brushed him aside he had shown his teeth in a mocking smile, as if to say: 'No wonder you won't talk.'

It was therefore a time to put up a good front, to

wear the mask of confidence. This was not the moment for looking harassed or taken aback. But as soon as I walked into the Ambassador's room, I knew that he had no mask to wear. He *was* harassed, and he *was* taken aback; and it showed all over his silly face.

I saw him alone. The Staff Security man, Blaustein, had offered to 'take me in'; when I said that I was capable of walking through a door alone, he turned sulky and muttered something about protocol. Apparently he had heard about the demotion. But I wasn't going to accept that. Within the Security Branch, Blaustein was still far junior to me; the fact that I was only a Third Secretary on Ambassador Black's staff wasn't going to alter that. After a brief tussle, I told him to shut up, and went in alone.

Ambassador Black, seated behind his desk in the long panelled room, looked exactly what he was; a small man out of his depth. I knew enough about him to wish that we had a better man in charge at this moment. He was not a career diplomat; he was a politician who, at a certain turn of the wheel, felt that he needed a prestige job and had enough friends to make sure that he got it. Now he had the prestige, but he hadn't the experience, and he hadn't the basic guts to deal with a Smith-and-Jones situation. By a freak of chance, the heat was on, the probe was in; and all he wanted to do was to duck his head and run for cover, back to politics, back anywhere.

His very first remark made this clear. It was a classic attempt at disengagement.

'I must say,' he said, in a high nervous voice, 'you people are sending us some very peculiar specimens, these days.'

I didn't feel ready to answer that sort of thing yet. When the time came to shoot it down, I would do my best. Instead I said:

'Sir, I'd like to be brought up to date. We haven't got a great deal to go on, at the moment. What's the present position?'

'The present position is that there is no position.' Ambassador Black paused, and looked at me as people do when they feel they have made an acute remark, and invite the world to share it. When I did not react, he frowned, and went on: 'I mean that, literally. . . . Smith and Jones disappeared from their apartment about four days ago, so far as we can tell. We don't know if they took their clothes, because there's a police guard on the building and we can't get in. I imagine the whole thing was prearranged, but it might have been a matter of impulse.' His lip curled briefly. 'They're an impulsive couple. . . . We reported them missing. We heard nothing at all until the official communiqué, saying that they had asked for political asylum.'

'Where are they now?'

'I don't know.'

'But have you made inquiries?'

'Of course I've made inquiries!' he said irritably. 'Good God, do you think we're asleep here? We've tried to see them. We've made every effort. Blaustein has spent hours down at the Foreign Affairs building. The answer is always no. All that these people will say is that Smith and Jones have put in this application, and while it's being considered, they cannot be interviewed by anyone. Being considered!' He blew out his cheeks. 'Of course they'll jump at the chance to get them. All they want to do is to make the biggest propaganda splash they can. Then we'll be told that Smith and Jones have been graciously accepted as refugees. And been given fat jobs as a reward. It makes you sick!'

I wished that he were a more stable character, but I had to do the best I could with the material available. I came back to a point which had caught my attention.

'You said that they disappeared from *their* apartment. Were they living together?'

'Oh yes! Very convenient arrangement.' His tone was an unpleasant sneer. 'I must say that I didn't expect you people to send us a prize pair like that. It's not our fault if this sort of thing happens. How can we guard against it? We can't watch our own staff twenty-four hours a day. We shouldn't have to watch them at all. Whoever cleared them ought to be shot.' His eyes sharpened; he had an important point to make. 'I hear it was you.'

I decided the time had come to bat this back. I had been travelling for nearly twenty-four hours; I was short of sleep, and not too sure of my ground. But this manoeuvre of Ambassador Black's was something which had to be scotched at the outset. He wasn't going to put the whole blame on to me. Bellinger had done it, so far, because he was in a position to. But this was the actual battlefield; the Embassy was the core of it, and the Ambassador had his own questions to answer. He must have.

'Whoever cleared them did it a year ago,' I said, as crisply as I could. 'When they're *en poste*, they are a local responsibility. That's in the regulations. Unless we are kept up to date, we have nothing to go on.' I put the decisive question. 'Was their disappearance the first sign of anything out of the ordinary?'

The Ambassador swallowed before answering. It was not going to take long to deflate him. 'Well—no.'

'You mean, you had some suspicions?'

'No, no,' he protested. 'I didn't say that at all. All I meant was that—that there had been a few irregularities.'

'Were they reported to anyone? I didn't see anything on the file.'

'Well—no,' said Ambassador Black again. 'Actually I was waiting. Waiting for something more definite. I don't want to go running home with every little thing.'

I said: 'You have something more definite now.'

'I couldn't possibly foresee *that*,' he said sulkily.

'We might have foreseen it, if we had been given the facts. I'd like to hear them now.'

With that, the story came out at last. It was very

much what I had been expecting. It showed clearly that Ambassador Black, perhaps to present a picture of a well-run Embassy, perhaps in the simple pursuit of a quiet life, had narrowed his eyes till they were scarcely open at all.

Smith (the Ambassador said) had been a bit of a puzzle at the time of his arrival. His colleagues had been expecting someone upset and even distraught by his wife's actions in London—the deserted husband of fiction if not of fact; they had been ready to show sympathy. Instead they found an affable, urbane man who seemed absolutely unaffected by what had happened to him. He was cheerful at all times; if he missed his wife, it was not at all apparent; and he never spoke about her save to answer formal inquiries outside the office, when he would say simply that she was 'getting better'. His bachelorhood, officially explained away by illness, caused no public comment at all. Very soon he had settled down to work and, within acceptable limits, to play.

He was an excellent host, and in this regard was an asset to the Embassy. His apartment became something of a party centre, rather chic, distinctly civilized; the fact that he made no women friends at all, and obviously preferred male company, seemed natural and even desirable, since it avoided the risk of scandal. Ambassador Black had known quite a few men who, abandoned by their wives, had gone right off the rails, causing all sorts of uproar. He had thanked God that there was nothing like this about Smith.

Then, for no apparent reason, Smith had started to deteriorate. He grew erratic, and even more careless in his dress, and seemed to lose interest in his work. There were more parties than ever, but they were of a rougher type; drinking bouts, all-night card sessions where too much money changed hands, noisy three-hour dinners in restaurants and hotels which had the other guests staring. The police had been called to his apartment twice, following complaints about noise. Smith had a grand piano, and he used to play it whenever the mood took him. His touch, apparently, was on the heavy side—too much so for apartment life.

I asked Ambassador Black if he had spoken to Smith about all this.

'Oh yes,' he answered. 'I certainly told him to take it easy.'

'Nothing more than that?'

Ambassador Black shrugged. 'What can you do? It's so damned dull here. I don't blame people for breaking out, now and then. And Smith was popular. Don't make any mistake about that. He threw these parties because he had a lot of friends who liked him. If they got out of hand, it wasn't exactly his fault.'

'Perhaps he was lonely.'

The Ambassador stared. 'How could he be, with all those people?'

I let it go. 'Then what?'

Then Jones arrived.

His reputation had preceded him; Ambassador Black had been expecting all sorts of fireworks, and was ready to do some straight talking. But Jones was very quiet, almost chastened; the 'two minutes' silence for Eichmann' affair in Israel had brought him very close to the limit of official patience; it seemed that he wanted to live it down, to reform, to make a new start. The Ambassador had nothing to complain of; in fact, he had *liked* Jones—a cheerful, well-mannered young man, a wonderful fetcher-and-carrier at Embassy parties. Of course, he was a bit—well, affected, but that didn't prove anything.

Then, after a few quiet weeks, Jones had moved into Smith's large apartment.

'We should have been told about that,' I commented.

'They said it was to save money.'

'They both get a rent allowance. There's no saving there.'

'Well, anyway—after that, Jones just seemed to break out.'

'Break out?'

The Ambassador looked away from me. 'I was going to write to you people about Jones.'

Immediately after the move, it seemed, things had started to hum; and Jones especially had reverted to his old form. To begin with, the habit of making quotable remarks on anyone and anything returned in full force. His reputation for this quickly became deplorable.

Of the wife of the Dean of the Diplomatic Corps, a massive woman whose amply-displayed bosom was the delight of local connoisseurs, he had remarked (in her hearing): 'It's lucky she's covered by diplomatic immunity.' He made an apt and spiteful comment about the British head-of-mission: 'He looks like a St. Bernard who's lost his brandy cask.' He was quoted as saying, of the local Federal elections, that they were occasionally interesting because there wasn't enough apathy to go round. He had profoundly embarrassed a mixed dinner party by declaring, in a chance moment of silence: 'Progress in the Foreign Service is either vaginal or rectal. You marry the boss's daughter or you crawl up his bottom.'

There were many more such things; there seemed to be a new 'Jones story' every day. People began to bait him at parties, in the hope of prompting something outrageous. They were rarely disappointed— under the sun of attention, he seemed to open out like a little poisonous flower. With the parties and the limelight, of course, went drinking. Celebrations in the Smith-Jones ménage became a diplomatic by-word. Jones was discovered in the lavatory, incapably drunk, at one Government reception; he smashed up his car, and did substantial damage to property, on another occasion.

He had been spoken to, he had been admonished, he had been disciplined. Always he promised to behave himself. Always he came up with some new outrage, almost before the echoes of the last one had died down.

Finally, and quite recently, there had been the affair of the film show, when he had made a public spectacle of himself and, more important still, had brought the Embassy into disrepute. At one of our receptions, before a distinguished gathering, Jones was to show a short prestige film, about the building of one of our biggest dams. The audience, well wined and dined, had settled itself in the Embassy drawing-room; the lights had been lowered; and the film came on—backwards.

On a different occasion, it might have been very funny. But this was not that sort of night, and the impression was disastrous. First there was the immense completed dam, stark and uncompromising, planted between the valley slopes; then the half-constructed concrete wall, and the half-ruined countryside; then the view gradually softened to the meandering river and the sylvan banks, and peace returned.

Instead of stopping the film, Jones had let it run, and then jumped up half-way through and said: 'Doesn't it look better this way?' The fact that there was a germ of truth in the remark only made it worse. In the ensuing silence, he had giggled wildly, and the audience, having no choice, giggled in answer. But there were too many nationalities for the joke to come off. What was funny for some was vaguely insulting to others, and an exhibition of futility to a third group. All in all, the evening was a total loss.

'That was pretty well the last straw, as far as I was concerned,' said Ambassador Black. 'I really blew him up, I can tell you. . . . I was going to write home and ask for a relief. But well—I left it for a week or so, and then—' he gestured, 'this thing happened.'

'Without any other warning?'

'Absolutely! Frankly, I think he's off his head. And Smith too.'

The recital of stupidities was over; the man who seemed to me to have committed more than his fair share of them sat staring at me across his desk, as if waiting for absolution. I would never have given it to him; Ambassador Black had been a damned fool.

A smart child of ten could have guessed that Smith and Jones were going to the bad; and that when they came together, the rate of progress would be doubled. Their first—their very first—joint indiscretion should have got them shipped straight home, without five minutes wasted in argument. The Ambassador must have been half asleep. Blaustein had shown himself equally gullible. . . . However, there was nothing to be gained by making any of these points. It wasn't a matter of laying the blame and chopping the necessary heads. My only concern was Smith and Jones.

I still had a few more points to be cleared up.

'There are a lot of gaps in this,' I told the Ambassador. I wasn't going to call him 'sir'. I wasn't going to call anyone 'sir' until I was back in circulation. 'Misconduct is one thing, treason is another. . . . If this *is* treason, and not just some damn-fool drunken joke. . . . Did they ever say anything about crossing over?'

'Not that I know of.'

I was in the mood to say that this didn't answer my question, but I held off. There might still be a few worthwhile facts to be gleaned.

'Did they ever complain about anything?' I went on. 'Did they ever say they'd had a raw deal? Were there any internal quarrels—office quarrels? Did either of them come into collision with any of your own people? What about your Minister? I suppose he was *Chargé d'Affaires* when you were on leave. Did he ever try to discipline them? Did he put in an adverse report?'

Faced with the quick-fire questions, Ambassador Black had been slowly shaking his head from side to side. When I paused, he answered:

'Honestly, there was nothing like that. They got on all right with the staff. I told you, people *liked* them. . . . Jones used to say that he wasn't getting anywhere, but hell!—everyone talks like that. And of course he *wasn't* getting anywhere. Why should he, the way he behaved? Smith never said anything on those lines, that I can recall.'

'Were they short of money?'

'They say Smith lost a lot at poker. Jones—I don't know. They must have spent plenty on drink. But that's duty-free, after all.'

'Any suspicious contacts?'

'No. Of course they knew a lot of people. They knew everybody. But they never seemed to have any particular friends. It was just a collection of people who liked parties.' He paused, and thought it over. After a while he said: 'I suppose they were just fed up.'

It might have been the first accurate statement Ambassador Black had made. It was, in truth, all that I had to go on; inquiry must start from there. If I could find out why they had crossed over, it might be the first step towards getting them back. It seemed likely, at the moment, that Jones was the instigator, the vicious spark to all this; he had the least to lose, because he was the nearest to being sacked. And he was that sort of young man; what a priest might have called an occasion of sin in others.

Smith could have gone along with him because he was lonely, and depressed, and (as his wife had never failed to remind him) he was not getting anywhere, either. But what this did to the chance of bringing him back, I could not even guess.

Ambassador Black, echoing my secret thoughts, remarked almost brightly:

'Well, what next?'

There was a knock at the door, and Blaustein entered, nearly running. Without looking at me, he said: 'Official hand-out, sir. Smith and Jones,' and laid a yellow flimsy in front of the Ambassador. After glancing at it, the Ambassador tossed it over to me.

It was a press release from the Ministry of Foreign Affairs. It was only two sentences long. It said that Smith and Jones, 'the two diplomats who have asked for asylum,' had been accepted as political refugees. They would hold their first press conference to-morrow morning at ten o'clock.

Ambassador Black, his face dispirited, said:

'I guess that answers my question.'

Six

You have to hand it to those people. When they put on a show, it's a show.

The Smith and Jones press conference was staged—and there was no other word—in the big committee-room of the Foreign Affairs building. It was a lofty hall, decorated with the busts of the great and with garish propaganda murals. There was a platform at one end; on this was a long table, and a dozen chairs, and a whole battery of radio and recording micro-phones. Film and television cameras lined the three other walls of the room; in the centre were about a hundred chairs for the audience. It was obvious that all the chairs were going to be needed.

Of course this thing had been building up in the press for nearly a week; even so, I was surprised at the number of correspondents from all over the world who had crowded into the conference room. Waiting for the show to begin, they were still milling around, crossing from row to row, talking, arguing, reading newspapers or scribbling down their background stuff. The uproar of their conversation resounded from the high ceiling. Powerful lights were being switched on and off as the camera-men lined up their equipment; photographers walked to and fro, working out angles, or focusing on a fat, bald official who had been posed in the centre chair to act as a dummy target.

Here and there was a silent man, a glum face, a disdainful or withdrawn expression; it marked one of our own correspondents, who did not expect to enjoy himself. But mostly this was a room full of cheerful and excited people. They had come for the fun, and they knew they were going to get it.

I sat with Blaustein, near the back of the room, staring straight ahead, not talking. We had been photographed half a dozen times on entering and when we took our seats; now we were trying to look neither happy nor unhappy, but blank. In this room, we were the outnumbered enemy. It was not going to be a good day for our side, and I wasn't going to give away anything extra in the way of copy.

In truth, I had plenty to think about. In spite of the years of training, and the occasional crises of the past, I was nervous. Smith and Jones were a great propaganda prize, as the room full of people showed; the next hour, whether they performed well or ill, was only going to confirm this. But they were valuable in other ways, too; valuable for what they had actually learned in their jobs, and for what they might choose to disclose.

Jones knew our cultural information pattern, and what we were really trying to do with this particular arm. He could be embarrassing to us, but not fatally so; things like that could be changed. Smith on the other hand had worked in a much more sensitive area; he had a picture of the positive future, which we did *not* want to change. If he started to talk, whether from malice, or from hope of reward, or to impress his hosts, it could be a serious setback.

Jones was the frosting on the cake. The cake—the really worthwhile captive—was Ivan Percival Smith.

There was a stir in the main doorway, and a parting of the crowd there. The big Klieg lights came on and began to blaze; shutters clicked and flash-bulbs exploded; conversation fell so quickly to nothing that the small whirring of the film-cameras could be heard. Smith and Jones appeared, blinking up at the fierce lights, hesitating in the doorway. They were motioned forward, and then led to the platform, by a tall black-suited man, smooth and oily—but smooth and oily like a shark—whom I knew as one of their senior Security men, Major Tollman.

A burst of clapping broke out as they came into view at the head table. They both bowed, smiling. Then they sat down.

I had plenty of time to study them during the next few minutes, while they posed for the photographers, and other officials sat down at the table, and an interpreter sidled in and took a seat between the two main actors. They could be observed at leisure. As far as I was concerned, it was hard on the stomach.

They were loving the limelight; they were both turned towards the warmth, like sunflowers. I had expected them to be pale, or nervous; they were two of the most collected people I have ever seen in public. Smith, though dressed with his usual sloppiness, was the very picture of heavyweight charm and consequence; a sort of unco-ordinated Oscar Wilde, florid, full of fruity self-confidence. Jones looked like one of those young men you see on the covers of Italian high-fashion magazines; small, foppish, barbered to the last eighth of an inch, a miniature of sunny elegance. Even the dark smudges under his eyes seemed appropriate to the picture, as if smudges were part of this year's younger man's make-up.

They turned their heads this way and that as the photographers called out to them. Everyone round them was smiling; Major Tollman was now a different kind of shark—a beaming shark, poised up and over for an easy kill. Jones leant across to say something to Smith, and Smith, raising heavy-lidded eyes, smiled back at him as if they were sharing the best private joke in the world. I could almost hear him saying: 'Suaviter in modo, dear boy.'

A man in the row in front of us, whom I recognized as one of our own senior correspondents, said disgustedly: 'Christ—where's the bucket?' That was my own reaction. But we were swimming against the tide. It was going to be very hard to puncture this.

The popping of flash-bulbs ceased gradually, the movement at the platform table subsided. Major Tollman nodded to Smith, then to Jones, then stood up. The entertainment began.

They kept it short, after all; the official transcript gives the best comprehensive picture, and it is the one I prefer to use. It is a general translation, of course; there were at least four languages used in this cosmopolitan circus. It does not name individual correspondents, though their affiliations are usually clear enough from the text. (A few of the questions stemmed from an early morning press briefing at our Embassy.) Above all, it doesn't convey what Smith and Jones looked like, what their mannerisms were— Smith's massive self-assurance, Jones's darting, brittle movements of head and arm; the overwhelming confidence (perhaps medically boosted for this occasion) which made them unable to resist the swift comeback, the smart piece of repartee.

But it was an accurate record. It was all I had to go on, for many weeks thereafter. And all in all, one must admit, it reflected a glittering performance.

Here it is:

TOLLMAN: I feel I need not introduce Mr. Smith and Mr. Jones. (*Laughter.*) We all know that they are here, and I may say that they are very welcome. I am going to ask them to tell you *why* they are here. Then they will be glad to answer questions.

SMITH: Thank you, Major Tollman. I have prepared a statement because I want to get this absolutely right. There is bound to be a good deal of misrepresentation of what we have done, in certain parts of the world; for that reason, and because we are not ashamed of our actions, I want to put our case, as simply and honestly as I can.

This statement falls into two parts; one is personal, and the other I might call ethical. On the personal side, I want to make it clear that this is not an act of impulse, nor the result of pique. We have both given this a lot of thought for a long time. We have grown dissatisfied with a large number of things about our jobs; in particular, we were ordered to do and say a large number of things which we do not believe in. In addition, we found a complete lack of freedom, and lack of opportunity, in our Foreign Service; we never seemed to be getting anywhere, and gradually we became convinced that only in a different setting, only in a totally different society, would we be able to fulfil ourselves. That is why we have taken this tremendous step.

So much for the personal side. The other part of my statement concerns much larger issues. Frankly, we came to the conclusion that we were living, and working, on the wrong side of the world. We have come to believe that what our own country is doing in the present world struggle is wrong, and immoral, and undesirable —not to mention unsuccessful. (*Laughter.*) No honest man can work for what he does not believe in. So we decided that we would not work for our country any longer. All we want to do now is to give all our energies to *your* country, and to help it, to the utmost of our ability, in its struggle for a peaceful solution to world problems, for a just and equitable world society.

If that means we are to be called traitors, it cannot be helped. But I would rather be called a traitor than a puppet or a dummy—and that is all we were, doing things we did not believe in when someone else pulled the strings. Now we are looking forward to a new life, and if someone else is still going to be pulling the strings, which happens in the best-regulated societies—(*Laughter*) at least we can be sure that the hand on the string is honest and capable, and its motives are peaceful and honourable. (*Applause.*)

I think that is all I want to say, except to emphasize two things: we are not in the least ashamed of what we have done, and we look forward with tremendous enthusiasm, as well as a sense of relief, to doing useful work in a useful society. For me, this moment is like being born again. You may think that I am a rather large baby, but I can assure you at least that my crying days are over. (*Laughter.*) That is all I want to say. Thank you for listening to me. (*Applause.*)

JONES: I don't think I need to make a statement. My eloquent friend has said it all for me. I've really nothing to add except to say what a relief it is to have taken this step at last. It is the first time in my life I have felt really free. (*Applause.*)

TOLLMAN: Thank you, gentlemen. May I say that, from our side, we are delighted to welcome you, and we are sure that you will never regret it, as long as you live. Now, are there any questions?

Q: Can you tell us some more about what was so unsatisfactory in your old life?

SMITH: Certainly. It was like being in prison. I don't expect that to mean anything to anyone here (*Laughter*) so I will elaborate. When one is set to do senseless tasks, and one cannot argue about them, and there is no escape from them, and no end to them—that is prison, to me.

Q: Could you explain 'senseless tasks'?

SMITH: Things I didn't approve of. (*Laughter.*) Oh yes, I admit I'm an egotist. (*Laughter.*) But of course there is much more to it than that. I thought all our policies were absolutely wrong— our foreign policy, our internal policy, our armaments policy, the whole range. This was the only way to escape, to make a clean break.

Q: Could you not have resigned?

SMITH: I would still be living in an environment and a tradition which I have come to despise.

Q: Is that what the word 'prison' means to Mr. Jones, too?

JONES: What's the point of that question?

Q: I understand you spent some time in prison in Belgrade.

TOLLMAN: I do not think that is relevant to what we are talking about today.

JONES: Oh, let him bring it up if it amuses him. Newspaper work must be so dull. I spent exactly one night—less, about six hours—in a police station in Belgrade after a traffic accident. It took that amount of time for our Embassy to arrange my release. Yugoslavia is not the world's most up-to-date country. (*Laughter*.) If that brands me as a convict, I'm ready to accept the label.

Q: May I ask how long you have known each other?

SMITH: About five years, on and off.

Q: Did you plan this thing together?

SMITH: I suppose you could say that, yes.

Q: But whose idea was it?

SMITH: It was a joint idea.

JONES: It comes under the heading, 'Great minds think alike'. (*Laughter*.)

Q: How long had you been planning it?

SMITH: It wasn't so much planning it as feeling it. We were both dissatisfied, we were both unhappy with what we were asked to do. Neither of us was getting anywhere, because the system simply does not allow it. It is utterly sterile, utterly point-less. We might as well have been two squirrels in a cage. You can see that I am no squirrel. (*Laughter.*)

Q: But why were you not getting anywhere?

SMITH: It's a long story. Let us say that the conditions of employment are extremely frustrating. They tend to reward plodding industry rather than imagination or intelligence. There is absolutely no place for a man who wants to think for him-self.

Q: Was this frustration anything to do with lack of promotion?

SMITH: Slowness of promotion, yes.

Q: Had that anything to do with your record?

SMITH: I do not understand you.

Q: I'm not talking to you, especially. Isn't it true that Mr. Jones has been in and out of trouble all his—

(*Confused interruption.*)

TOLLMAN: I think we have already dealt with that, perfectly adequately. Next question.

Q: May I have an answer?

JONES: I'm not afraid to answer. Why should I be? Of course I've been in trouble. Who hasn't? A man who never makes mistakes never makes anything. It's precisely because I was picked on and hounded for every single mistake, every little infringement of the rules, every time I said 'No, sir,' instead of 'Yes, sir,' that I'm in this room today. I can't stand that sort of atmosphere, I don't believe it exists in this country, and I've come here to prove it. (*Applause.*)

Q: Was there any pressure on you to make this change?

SMITH: How could there be?

Q: I am asking you.

SMITH: Not at any time.

Q: Any question of blackmail?

SMITH: I am not subject to blackmail.

Q: Nor Mr. Jones?

SMITH: I do not see where this is leading. There was no pressure of any sort from anyone. This was and is our free choice.

Q: Have you had access to secret material?

SMITH: I cannot answer that question.

Q: Are you going to sell it?

SMITH: You are in a position to be offensive. I will not try to compete with you.

TOLLMAN: We will take the next question.

Q: Have you been promised jobs?

SMITH: We have been promised nothing.

Q: What do you expect to live on?

JONES: Hope. (*Applause.*)

Q: Mr. Smith, you spent eight months as a prisoner in Korea?

SMITH: Yes.

Q: Were you brain-washed?

SMITH: I must confess that I do not know what that peculiar phrase means.

Q: Did your time there make any difference to you?

SMITH: Yes. I lost ten pounds. (*Laughter.*)

Q: May we have a proper answer?

SMITH: I am sorry. I did not mean to be improper. (*Laughter.*) What was the question, please?

Q: Did your time as a prisoner in Korea lead to this decision?

SMITH: No. It was over ten years ago. It had nothing whatever to do with this.

Q: What is your position on nuclear testing?

JONES: I hope I would be underground. (*Laughter.*) I haven't given it a lot of thought. I suppose it is necessary.

SMITH: It may be essential.

Q: Essential for one country and not for another?

SMITH: That may quite possibly be true. If you feel that you are being ringed around by enemies, or that one particular enemy is prepared to go to any lengths to destroy you and all that you stand for—then I think you are entitled to test and to perfect any weapons at your disposal.

Q: And to use them?

SMITH: Not necessarily. History proves that all new weapons have *not* been used. Poison gas has never been used seriously. Germ warfare has never been used. It is my hope that thermo-nuclear weapons will never be used in war. But one is entitled to have them ready, and to use them as a lever for bargaining.

Q: Are both sides entitled?

SMITH: Yes, I suppose so. But there is absolutely no doubt in my mind as to which country is likely to be the aggressor, and which is on the defensive.

Q: Do you mean that your own country—perhaps I should say your ex-country—is the aggressor?

SMITH: Unquestionably. It is in the very air we breathe, it is the stuff we are fed daily. You have only to read the newspapers. That is one reason, and a very strong one, why I am so glad to have escaped from it.

Q: Will your wife be joining you here?

SMITH: No.

Q: Why not?

SMITH: You know women. (*Laughter.*)

TOLLMAN: Are there any more questions?

Q: May we congratulate Mr. Smith and Mr. Jones on a courageous decision? (*Applause.*)

Q: May we do nothing of the sort? (*Applause.*)

JONES: May we have a drink? (*Loud laughter.*)

Seven

THEY were the undoubted heroes of the hour. There was absolutely nothing we could do except sit back and watch them wolfing their cake.

I tried to see them, and failed; they were granting no interviews except those screened by the Security people, and certainly none to their ex-colleagues. We could, if we wished, join the admiring throng as they moved about the city; or watch them on television; or write to them. . . . It seemed better to hold off until the climate had cooled.

From the propaganda point of view, they were being handled very well; in those first few weeks they made a fantastic impact. I suspected that Tollman's was the guiding hand here. He knew what a prize he had, in Smith and Jones; he knew just how much profit he would get out of them, in the short and the long run; he knew the pace to start and the pace to finish. It was a first-class professional job.

The starting pace was brilliantly planned; having secured his prizes in a blaze of publicity, Tollman now gave them just enough scarcity value to stoke the fire. He did not throw them on the market, as a lesser man might have done; he carefully rationed them, so that each public appearance was a separate and sensational event.

First there was a nation-wide television interview, a sort of miniature of the press conference; but this time the interviewers were carefully chosen, and the questions angled with skill. Smith and Jones emerged not simply as refugees, but refugees from a crushing tyranny which threatened to extinguish the spark of freedom within the human breast, wherever that breast might be. It was a beautiful bit of nonsense; and it was tremendously successful.

The next event, a few days afterwards, was social; the *première* of the Peking Ballet Company, at the start of its national tour. Smith and Jones attended, and made a late entrance to one of the stage boxes; from the public reaction, they might have been two favourite princelings in a country which still worshipped royalty. Smith wore a magnificent silk-lined opera cloak (I noticed that they were making him dress much better, a thing we had never been able to do); Jones sported a frilled shirt front, and a dinner-jacket which seemed to be made of cloth of gold.

They were, of course, the sensation of the evening.

In the interval they held court, while the glittering audience focused its collective stare on them, and earned an occasional gracious wave of the hand. The Ballet Company might just as well have stayed in Peking. Gossip said that Jones was lost backstage for three hours after the performance, but I was sure the story was malicious. Major Tollman had him much too well chaperoned for that.

After this there was a public banquet of welcome, at which it was announced that in view of their talents, unrecognized in their own country, Smith and Jones were being assigned to important (though unspecified) work in the Ministry of Foreign Affairs. They were mobbed afterwards, with such noisy realism that I was almost convinced that this was a demonstration of genuine public acclaim.

Then there was silence for a week. 'Extreme pressure of work' was the official version, which went on to explain that so intense was their enthusiasm that they had asked to be employed straight away. I imagined that they were being interrogated, not too insistently. Tollman had plenty of time.

Smith then emerged to open an exhibition of contemporary art, and made an amusing and indeed quite learned speech on the decadence of artistic expression in his own country. Jones, moving into the same general field, wrote and recorded a calypso-type song about their defection. It was a catchy tune called 'Two Men say Yes! to Freedom'. He accompanied himself on the guitar; the result was an instant bestseller which had the populace whistling, humming, singing, and dancing for weeks afterwards. It was freely rumoured that this splendid talent of Jones's had hitherto been officially frowned on, and indeed suppressed, from motives of jealousy.

So it went on; by the end of the first month Smith and Jones were on the map in a dozen different ways, an established showpiece of man's eternal striving to escape from human bondage. As I said, we could only sit back and watch them eat it up. Truth to tell, they were doing just as good a job as Tollman; and, basking in this special limelight, the first of their lives, they were loving it.

All this time I was under my own share of lime-light, and not loving it at all. It was all very well to enjoy their performance, from the professional point of view; but within our Embassy, two things were being made clear; firstly, that I was the only one who was appreciating the saga of Smith and Jones, from any angle, and secondly that I bore the chief responsibility for it. In my many interviews with Ambassador Black, one point was continuously hammered home. I was 'in charge of' Smith and Jones. What was I doing about it?

'Waiting' was a feeble answer, but it was the best I could manage, at that particular moment. It did not sit well with Ambassador Black. When I used the word, he looked at me as if I had sworn at him.

'Waiting?' he repeated. 'Waiting for what?'

'To see how this thing develops.'

'We know how it's developing.' He gestured towards some photographs of Smith and Jones 'hard at work at their new desks', which were front-paged in the two principal newspapers. 'While you're *waiting*, these people are getting away with murder. They're building up to the biggest thing since man went into orbit.'

I looked at the photographs, lying on the desk between us. Smith, gazing straight at the camera, appeared positively statesmanlike; Jones, his pencil poised, was the very picture of an eager young diplomat with the world at his feet. The impression on the newspaper reader was one of earnest yet happy dedication.

'They're doing a good job,' I said.

'What do you mean, good job? It's a disgusting racket!'

'Oh yes.' He was confusing two different things. 'What I meant was, they're being handled very well and they are responding to it.'

'What I'd like to hear is how we're responding to it.'

He was looking at me angrily, as if I had got him into this embarrassment, and was wilfully failing to get him out of it again. That was his personal reaction; but he was thinking and speaking also for Colonel Bellinger, who was always there in the background, bearing down hard on all concerned, and especially on me. Ambassador Black was nothing, in this section of the story; Bellinger had the lead; he was the man I had to impress, and so far I had nothing to impress him with.

'I've made a lot of inquiries,' I told the Ambassador. It was better to give him something to chew on, rather than have him nagging all the time. 'I still can't get near them; they won't give interviews to anyone on our side, and they're too well guarded for a casual approach. But I've got a good idea of what's going to happen to them. They'll be sent on a cross-country tour, as soon as things quieten down, and then they'll come back here to live. They're going to move into one of the new suites at the International.'

'A government suite?' asked Ambassador Black. The International Hotel was where the government usually put its principal guests, whenever there was an official visit to the capital; they kept three or four floors permanently reserved. 'That means they'll still be under guard.'

'They'll be under guard for a long time. But we can still keep an eye and an ear on them.' I mentioned some technical arrangements I had organized. 'The electricians are working on that now.'

He was impressed, in spite of himself. 'You must be finding your way around,' he said.

'That's routine,' I answered, off-handedly. 'It'll be a sad day when I can't put a microphone into a newly decorated room, anywhere in the world. But that's as far as we can go, at this point. We'll watch them, and listen to them. One of these days I'll be making direct contact. But not yet.'

Ambassador Black began to frown again. He had been impressed by these small conjuring tricks, but he was not basically reassured. What he wanted was results, something to clear his record.

'That's very good, as far as it goes,' he said. 'But in the meantime, Smith and Jones are getting a long way ahead of us. What are the chances of bringing them back again? Persuading them that this is all wrong?'

'None, at present. Even if we could get through to them. They're enjoying themselves much too much. It's the first time they've *been* anybody. They don't think this is all wrong. They think it's wonderful.'

'Then isn't it time we made a few points ourselves? Shouldn't we say we're glad to be rid of them —something like that?'

'It won't cut any ice,' I told him. 'They're doing too well at the moment. You can't swim against that sort of tide.' I mixed another metaphor for him. 'Give them a bit more rope. They'll hang themselves.'

'But in the meantime,' he said again, 'we've got to live with the bastards.' His eyes became professionally narrow. 'How much have they told, do you think?'

'All they know.' From a number of sources, I was sure this was true, and I had so reported it. 'Jones has been singing like a bird. Not that he has much of a tune to sing, except that damned calypso. But Smith has been very co-operative.'

'That's bad,' said the Ambassador. He sighed gustily. 'Well, do the best you can. How are you getting along with Blaustein?'

'Well enough.' It was true; after a few contrary efforts, Blaustein had fallen into line. 'When Smith and Jones go on their tour, I'd like him to follow them, if he can get clearance for the trip.'

'What about you?'

'I want to get things organized here,' I answered. 'The tour is nothing, really; it'll just be a repeat performance of the arrival circus. This is where they're going to live, and this is where the fight will be. We've got to look a year ahead.'

'A year?' he repeated, dismayed. 'But what's going to happen in the meantime?'

'Let's say we have a year to kill.'

When I said that I wanted to get things organized here, I really meant that I wanted to look around. I was likely to stay a long time in this outlandish place. The sooner I was used to it, the better.

It is strange how one hates certain cities, certain countries, certain people. Of course, it can always be traced back a long way; back to the books and newspapers one has read, the chance encounters of a quarter of a century or more, the training one receives, the orders one carries out. I was a product of all these things, which ranged in distance and in quality from my mother's knee to Colonel Bellinger's desk; I was a product of the world about me, and of a moment of history which dictated that one half of that world must fear, hate, or deride the other half. I agreed with that dictation: no effort was involved: in fact it was a pleasure as well as a duty. Without any trouble, I hated this city, this country, this people.

To begin with, the weather was against any other reaction. Heaven knows it can be cold enough at home; but this searing, biting, sub-zero siege was something special to cope with. One had to dress up for it, as everyone else did; it involved fur caps, fur-lined coats, clumsy snow-boots, ear-muffs, windproof gloves. It was bitter, it was exhausting; to move about at all was an intolerable effort.

It never seemed to be that, at home. Perhaps this was only another aspect of my hatred, but it *was* real.

Cars, left unattended for an hour, promptly froze up; even the locks on the doors of cars froze up, so that one could not even get inside to try to spark some life into a dead engine. The roads were stretches of pounded-in, hammered-down, grimy snow; the pavements treacherous little skating rinks. Bundled up, one blundered on the city streets into other bundles, stamping, plodding, sliding, battling, as miserable and withdrawn as oneself. Sometimes it was like moving through a city of stumbling corpses, leaning drunkenly into the wind, soon to be swallowed up by the whirling snow.

It was a sprawling city, an architectural mess; fine

buildings, relics of a more lavish past, stood side by side with modern concrete boxes; a few yards away, behind this respectable façade, many of the streets seemed to crumble swiftly into new and old slums, shabby and ill-kept; by our standards, all of them were disgraceful derelicts, fit only for the wrecker's hammer. These people had tried—as in so many other things—to marry the past with the present; the result was a great nothingness of taste, an ugly illustration on an ugly page of history. And everywhere, that pervasive cold, sweeping across the frozen river, seemed to transfix the whole place in its disfigurement.

Cold like that does something to people, also. These people it had made suspicious, ungenerous, and dull. Or did this come from the food—monotonous, starchy, thickening the waist-line (it seemed) of every man and woman over twenty-five? Or did it come from their books and newspapers and magazines, all dedicated to one dreary theme which ruled all their thinking all their lives? Or did it come from their politics, so belligerent, so selfish, so grossly material— just as I had expected? Or did it, after all, come from the cold, as a simple blight of nature?

The catalogue could be endless; one ran out of adjectives; this was a wasteland of the dull, the prejudiced, the self-righteous, the wrong-headed. But I think it was their children I disliked most of all. I am not claiming that our own brats are perfect; the newspapers prove otherwise, every day. But there was something about these cocky, assertive, manner-less young animals which made me loathe them on sight.

Even these were the children of educated people, brought up in reasonable homes. There were others —gangs of teenage louts, vicious and uncontrollable— who terrorized whole districts of the city, and were perhaps the most hideous product of a conformist society. They had mutinied against the pattern. But they had not become free spirits. They had become brutes.

Finally, to complete this dreary picture, there was our own special position, as envoys from an enemy camp, staying there only until enmity ripened into aggression. Like all our diplomats in this part of the world, we were virtually walled up, like men living in a compound; we were isolated from all exchange, all normal contact, by the triple barriers of language, politics, and outlook. We were different—our clothes, our speech, our habits of life; we were foreigners of a distinctive kind, to be watched all the time because our motives could only be suspect.

We never got to know anybody, outside the diplomatic corps; perhaps most of us did not want to, but anyway, this was how it was; we lived in lonely quarantine. Our Ambassador knew other Ambassadors, to nod to or to toast on the endless clutter of 'National Days' (almost invariably celebrating freedom from the British yoke) which were customary in all capitals. Soldiers knew soldiers, on a rigid professional basis; men with binoculars focused them on their opposite numbers; policemen (under any label) saluted policemen.

There was here a force of policemen of the kind I respected; federal, secretive, possessors of the final word. I wished I could mix with these, my brothers in law. But I was a Third Secretary. I knew other Third Secretaries, and their little wives, and their little cars and homes and menus and cocktail *canapés*. I gave little parties, on the same modest basis. I kept an eye on Smith and Jones, via Blaustein's reports. I tried to keep warm, I thought and planned the future. I waited, not growing reconciled to anything or anyone.

That was all, until the illuminating day when I met Major Tollman, the most significant policeman of the lot.

It was the evening before Smith and Jones were due back in the capital. I was at one of the customary 'National Day' parties, celebrating yet another escape from the heel of the long-suffering British; this one was a first anniversary, and had been happily linked with a guaranteed British loan of ten million dollars a year for the next eight years. There were the usual toasts, the usual congratulations; the drinks were the same, the loaded buffet tables identical with those of the party the night before and, no doubt, the party the next night. Duty required the four guests from our mission, headed by Ambassador

Black, to remain for one hour. It was proving a long sixty minutes.

I was passing the time with a whisky and soda, and watching the Premier go through his customary party act; not for the first time, I reflected that he was really a great loss to the stage. He went from group to group throughout the long room, shaking hands, slapping backs, drinking toasts, exchanging jokes and twinkling smiles and broad gestures of amity and good fellowship. This was the international glad hand at its most expansive. What always astonished me (I had already watched him on a dozen occasions) was how his personality could react to whatever the current company required. It was true, political, quick-change artistry.

He was a farmer to another farmer—he even looked like one; he was a grave statesman when he was talking to Ambassadors; he was shrewd-eyed when he talked finance, hearty when he talked politics, roguish and bantering when he talked to the press. He could switch anger on, or cold politeness, or warm admiration; he could look relaxed with a drunkard, and positively ascetic with a Papal delegate. It was all as phoney as it could possibly be; but, in the realm of the counterfeit, it was marvellous.

I was watching it, and enjoying it, when presently I became aware that someone standing close beside me was also watching, not the Premier, but myself. I turned my head gradually, to meet his eyes. It was Major Tollman.

He nodded without hesitation, though we had never met, and said: 'Well, Mr. Third Secretary. . . . How are you enjoying yourself?'

His tone and his whole manner were ironic, as if we shared a secret, and we both knew we shared it. Close to, he was more shark-like than ever; the white teeth in the olive face, the white shirt against the dead-black suit, the strong sleek body, the tiny gleaming shoes which were themselves like a tail— all aided the illusion. But tonight he was an affable shark, and I was ready to talk to him on that basis. This was a man who was probably closer to me—in his thoughts, his professional intentions, his habits of work—than most other men. It suddenly struck me that I would rather be talking to Major Tollman than to Ambassador Black. It also struck me that, with Smith and Jones due back the next day, he might well have staged this encounter on purpose; and his very next words seemed to confirm this. Without preface, cutting many corners, he said:

'Not keeping a personal eye on our new friends?'

It was clearly better not to dissemble. It was also easier. I answered: 'I might say the same to you.'

'They don't need my eye!' He reached out a long hand to a passing tray, and took half a dozen sardines on tiny slivers of toast. Then he popped them into his mouth one by one, all the time looking at me. Live bait, I thought; the shark illusion was complete. . . . 'In fact, they don't seem to need anything, at the moment,' he went on. 'Doing very well. . . . Wonderful team. . . .' Suddenly, unexpectedly, he wrinkled his nose. 'Why do you employ people like that?'

We were backed into a corner, out of all the main eddies of the party; it was quite private. 'Why do you?' I asked in turn.

He laughed at that. There was something comradely and cordial in the laugh, as if he were glad that we both knew the score.

'Oh, they're an asset to *us*, all right. Jones's guitar alone is worth the money. And Smith is a very interesting man.' He put the last of the sardines into his mouth, still staring at me, and then licked his fingers one by one. 'Very interesting. Very talented. Very knowledgeable. I think we can use him.'

'I am sure that you have.'

He nodded for several moments. Then for the first time his eyes left my face, and roamed idly round the room. When he spoke, it was sideways to me, so that I could not see any expression, only hear the crisp confident voice setting out the ground-rules.

'Watch them as much as you like,' he said. 'But don't try to get them back. You won't do it.'

'Who wants them back?'

He ignored this. He was buttoning his coat, as if preparing to leave. 'As long as you're a Third Secretary,' he said, 'we're not worrying. But if you get ambitious, we'll have to say goodbye to you. At very short notice.'

That seemed fair enough; indeed, I was grateful for it. 'Is that official?'

'It's as official as it will ever be.' He turned round and held out his hand, unexpectedly. 'I must be off. I have two more of these damned things.' On the point of leaving me, he added one extra item, and it was not the least of that evening. 'By the way, we've saved ourselves some trouble, at your expense.'

I waited, sure that it would be worthwhile.

'Don't start worrying adout your impedance meters. We've hooked into your microphones.'

Eight

THEY settled down very quickly; it was made easy for them by a continuing popular welcome, and a benign official smile. Swiftly milked of all they knew, they had been rewarded with vague but well-paid 'liaison' jobs at the Ministry of Foreign Affairs; for though they were no longer directly useful to Major Tollman, their value as a propaganda prize remained. Thus they were now to be installed as public pets, two show-dogs of an unusual breed, one large, the other small, who had passed their obedience tests and were awarded the customary prize—three square meals a day and an ornamental rosette.

The rosette was the social life of the capital, into which they now dived with a prodigious splash. They were well-known personalities at last—the darlings of at least half the diplomatic corps, the objects of the close attention of the other half; they had never attracted so much notice in their lives, and they reacted to it with a zest which was, to me, revolting to watch. They were *the* celebrities; when they entered a room, they were immediately surrounded by a crowd which knew that Jones was sure to make a quotable comment, and that Smith would display a heavyweight charm which was an asset to any party.

At the theatre or the ballet or the symphony concert, they occupied prominent seats and became the centre of admiring attention before, during, and after the performances. For the New Year's Eve costume party given by a senior neutral Ambassador, Smith came dressed as the Emperor Nero, and Jones as a female slave. Though this was too strong for some stomachs, it earned wild applause, and the first prize —a case of champagne.

Jones did a lot of television work; Smith was said to be working on a translation of some Latin poems; their cultural contribution was thus established. Between this, and their official jobs, and the diplomatic receptions, and their own parties, and the peculiar notoriety which attended every move they made, they had achieved the sort of life which perhaps had been a cherished dream for both of them. Amazingly, it did not seem to be costing them anything, either.

Our eyes met, occasionally, as they were bound to; for diplomats, a capital city was only as big as the current reception room. Smith would turn away with a cold glance; but Jones would sometimes give me a curious lift of the head, a half smile, as if to say:

'Come on in—join the party—don't be left out.' Of course we never spoke, or indeed came within ten yards of each other. But I did not need to meet them, in order to know exactly what they were doing.

They were personally happy; there were too many pleasures, distractions, and triumphs in their new life to leave any time for quarrels. I did once send a girl in—as one sends a ferret into a rabbit warren—to see if she could start anything. Her instructions were to make a play for Smith, the ex-married man who might conceivably be lonely.

She was a big blonde slut (I had to guess at his tastes), who seemed ordinarily to have very little trouble in convincing men that they now had a wonderful chance to prove it. But after a week's steady siege, she gave me a decidedly negative report.

'There's nothing doing there,' she told me. 'He doesn't know I'm alive.'

'I'm surprised,' I said. 'You're a pretty girl.'

A grimace flickered across her smooth, corrupt face. 'Try a pretty boy.'

That seemed to dispose of that. It confirmed what one of our people on the staff of the International Hotel had told me. The Smith and Jones ménage was perfectly contented as it was.

There was one curious item of information which I puzzled over for a long time, and then filed away. Jones was getting money from home—a regular monthly allowance, paid into his bank. It was puzzling because of our currency regulations, which were still very strict and could only be by-passed in two ways: illegally, or as a matter of policy. I had no means of finding out which was true in this case, until Colonel Bellinger gave me a clue.

I had flown back to see him after completing six months' exile; nominally to make the sort of report which we did not commit even to coded cable traffic, actually to see what were my own prospects of release. It was impossible not to feel that I was wasting my time, and that I was being made to waste my time, as a matter of discipline; I guessed that the official policy—Colonel Bellinger's policy—was to tie me to Smith and Jones whatever happened, and that somewhere on my file was the notation: '*Seconded S. & J. indefinite.*' I didn't know what I could do about it, but I thought it was time to rebel a little. I had nothing much to lose; I could hardly be demoted further.

It was high summer, and wonderful to be home. But Colonel Bellinger gave me no hope that I could stay there. Inside the Security building, the temperature had not risen by a single degree.

Our session was a long one. I had to expand various written reports, answer a lot of queries, and give an estimate of the future. Bellinger questioned me closely on a whole range of subjects: the exact kind of work Smith and Jones were doing, what other diplomats they mixed with, whether they ever saw any of our own people, whether there had been any reaction from the first rush of popularity. He was especially inquisitive about my skirmish with Major Tollman, as he had every right to be. But when I steered the talk round to myself, he became, for the first time, non-committal. Perhaps 'uninterested' was a better word.

'We're satisfied with what you're doing,' he said. 'I can tell you that.'

He was looking at me with cold attention, as if he expected me to be overjoyed with this crumb of commendation. It was not at all what I was looking for.

'I'm not doing anything,' I said. 'Colonel, I don't want to question my orders, but this is really a complete waste of time, my staying with them. We'll never get them back. They're much too well off.'

He kept his eyes fixed on me, but it seemed that his glance had become less direct. After a long moment, he said: 'I'm not too sure that we want them back, now.'

'I don't understand.'

'It's the feeling here,' he answered—and he spoke as a man on the inside speaks to a man excluded— 'that this thing seems to be settling down. Smith and Jones have gone. The serious damage is done. The excitement is obviously dying away. We don't want to revive it.'

I thought quickly, decided that I had nothing to lose, and came straight out with the linking question, which had only just occurred to me.

'Does that explain the money from home?'

He nodded, as if a dull pupil had suddenly shown brightness above the average. 'Very possibly. I think we can say that Smith and Jones are perfectly happy where they are, and that some of their friends at home are perfectly happy also. But they—the friends —wouldn't like to think of Smith and Jones as having to worry about money.'

I was truly astonished, for the first time in this whole affair. 'But does this department have to go along with that sort of thing?'

He looked at me very coldly indeed. '*This depart-ment*,' he said, with special emphasis, as if I had a very slight connection with it, 'is executive. It does not make policy, it carries it out. I may say that since *this department* let Smith and Jones get away, we are hardly in a position to argue about our orders.' His finger-tips came together; it was the old, well-remembered sign of dismissal. He added, as a final blessing: 'Nor are you.'

It was an appalling setback. I had come into the room hoping to talk myself into an immediate change of jobs, or at least a promise of release; and suddenly, at a single stroke, I was worse off than ever. It seemed that I had no prospects at all; I had become part of a protection racket for people like Smith and Jones. They were to stay where they were for ever, and I was to be part of the entourage. . . . I made one more effort.

'But sir, doesn't that let me out? If they're going to be left as they are? What am I meant to be doing?'

'Keeping them under surveillance.'

'But for what purpose?'

'Keeping them under surveillance,' he repeated. 'I should not have to tell you that, wherever they are, their file will never be closed.' He stood up, a small insignificant figure, tough enough for me and for a lot of other people. 'You can take a week here, if you want to. I understand that you have to have a tooth out.'

I had not mentioned it; he could only had got the information from Blaustein. It rounded out a grim pattern.

'How long am I likely to be kept there?'

'As long as the present situation lasts.'

It lasted exactly a year, the year I had mentioned ambiguously to Ambassador Black; the year we had to kill, the year in which they had to kill themselves. They celebrated their first anniversary with a party, and from that moment they began to go steeply downhill. Since I had a score to settle, I was glad to watch the process. But it would have been interesting anyway.

It started in small ways; in fact, it started in one very small way, which alerted me to all the rest. I used to tune in to Jones's regular television show; I thought of it as part of my job, but in fact it was often worth watching, in a morbid sort of way. It was built around a ten-minute personal appearance, during which he sang his signature calypso, '*Two Men say*

Yes! to Freedom', with some topical verses added, played a guitar solo, told some jokes in extremely broken dialect, sang another song, and bowed out. But the occasion which I remember, as giving me the looked-for sign, was much shorter.

Jones was drunk on camera; not falling-down drunk, but stupid drunk. He came on stage rocking slightly, and there followed a very swift sequence. He forgot the lines of his signature tune, which tailed off into silence. Then he dropped his guitar, which can be a very noisy business. After a single expletive, he burst into giggling laughter. Then he was faded out.

It was a sudden indisposition, we were told by a smooth-toned announcer. Later they said that he had a high fever, and was performing directly against his doctor's orders. But it was the end of Jones on television, and perhaps the end of Jones.

I thought about it for many hours that night, with pleasure and speculation. Jones had never been publicly drunk before; the last significant occasion within my own knowledge was the time in Belgrade, when he had killed the woman, and wept in the Ambassador's study, and cried out: 'I was in despair.' It was good to think that he was in despair again, if that was the case.

The despair must have been triggered by something personal, which I never found out; what was easier to establish was that Smith and Jones were not the official darlings they once had been, and that a lot of people knew this, and that they knew it themselves. The cancellation of the television series meant that one segment of the limelight had been switched off. There were other signs, which could only mean that they were past the peak of their favouritism. And past that peak, there could only be one kind of slope.

Perceptibly the climate had begun to cool. Probably I was the first to notice, because I was looking for it; the man who finds the smell is the man who sniffs. This smell of failure showed itself in small things and in large. Before long it could not be disguised from anyone.

Smith's clothes, except on very formal occasions, grew sloppy and untidy again; he shambled about the city as if he did not care what impression he made. Jones quarrelled violently with a Western newspaperman at a press reception; his comments grew so savage and his behaviour so outrageous that he was asked to leave.

They began to be left out of things, or to be downgraded in a subtle way which would not register with ordinary people, but which was mortifying to anyone treading water in the deeper parts of the social sea. They were invited, not to State dinners, but to the larger receptions afterwards, a sort of overflow rag-bag of city councillors, very minor diplomats, and departmental committee chairmen; the shoulders they now rubbed were practically anonymous. As in public life, so in private; the dinner party for twelve distinguished guests gave way to the buffet supper for fifty, or, worse still, the cocktail party for two hundred. It was strange how the word spread. Suddenly they were poison, only to be tolerated with the maximum dilution.

I noted a dozen instances of the way in which they were slipping, of their failing grasp on popularity and rank. There were two, with which I had personal contact, which will serve to illustrate this fatal decline.

The first was at another ballet *première* in the capital, this time of the Royal Ballet Company from England, which we were ready to greet, it seemed, just as happily as their Peking *confrères*. It was very much an invited audience; such diplomats as could afford it wore their official uniforms and decorations; the women had done their best or their worst in the way of jewels and finery; the Premier was escorting a visiting African President whose cheerful face beamed and sweated above a magnificent purple-and-gold-thread mantle which must indeed have been excessively hot.

Smith and Jones made their entrance—and the contrast with their triumphal appearance of the first week in the capital was ludicrous. Faultlessly dressed for the occasion, they marched forward practically to the footlights, smiling and bowing, and handed their tickets to an usher. He looked at the cards, held them up to the light, and then began to march back again, motioning Smith and Jones to follow him.

Back and back they went, in crestfallen retreat; past the cream of the official seats, past the solid phalanx of the middle ground, past the line of the balcony overhead, back into the shadowy outer circle. When the usher finally stopped, three rows from the rear exit, Smith and Jones were almost as far back as I was. It must have been horrible for them.

Smith, splendid in his opera cloak, was still managing a tight smile, but Jones was clearly furious. After a short argument with the usher, they sat down, and began to whisper to each other. Then Jones jumped up again, saying (according to a nearby informant): 'Obviously there's been some mistake. I'll soon fix this!' Then he flounced down the aisle, and out into the lobby.

It was quite a long time before he came back, and the house lights were gradually dimming. But there was still light enough to see his face, a small but positive thundercloud. They did not move their seats, and they left after the first interval.

The second instance was more revealing still—or rather, it revealed much more of their own thoughts, their reaction to the loneliness of disfavour. It was also quite moving, if you were of a sort likely to be moved by the sight of justice being done, or believed that criminals should escape all due penalties.

Smith had to make a speech. Such occasions were now rare, and gained little space or attention in the newspapers; this particular one had the usual connotations of culture—a dinner meeting of provincial librarians, at which Smith was the guest of honour and Jones came along to keep him company and, it was observed, to dispose of most of a bottle of wine. It should have been a dull and decorous affair.

After the speech, a modest effort dedicated to the proposition that books were good things, and reading them was a more rewarding habit than dancing or watching football, there was a question period. Somehow, this led Smith to make a sudden manifesto on a personal theme. It was not what the good librarians had come to hear, but it certainly held their attention.

It was sparked by an innocuous question as to what particular work, in the literary field, Smith was engaged on now. He answered, fairly off-hand, that he was doing translations of various kinds. Then he paused in thought, for a long minute, as if trying to make up his mind. Then he suddenly lifted his head, and said:

'I wish I had more to do.' He gestured towards Jones. 'I wish we both had more to do. We've been here more than a year, as most of you know. It cost us a great deal, one way and another, to make the change. I sometimes wonder whether it was worth while.' There was already an utter stillness in the room; the chairman of the dinner, frowning in embarrassment, was looking up at Smith, trying to catch his eye, but Smith was seeing nothing but himself, and Jones, and the wall of their joint miseries. 'Of course we love this country, and we can never regret what we have done. But I had hoped—' he hesitated, '—I had expected that there would be more recognition of the sacrifices we have made, in order to stay here.'

He paused again: the stillness thickened all over the room; Jones was seen to have dropped his head in his hands, as if struck by sudden despair. The chairman said: 'Are there any more questions?'

'I have not quite finished,' said Smith, in his coldest, grandest, most impressive manner. 'I said that we loved this country, and it is true. We are ready to do anything for it. We have already done a great deal, suffered a great deal, put up with all sorts of disappointments and slights and insults. . . . What we *won't* do is to let all this effort, this ordeal, go to waste. To be forgotten. To be passed over. To be buried. I would rather—'

The chairman plucked up his courage at last, and interrupted him. 'This is not quite relevant to the meeting,' he said, with slightly desperate determination. 'I think that we should perhaps—'

Now it was his turn to be interrupted, this time by Jones. Jones raised his head, and the reason why he had bowed it became apparent; he was crying, or starting to cry. Tears glistened in his eyes as he suddenly burst out:

'It *is* relevant! It's relevant to everything in this whole damned world! Do you know what my distinguished and scholarly friend—' (he was quoting, savagely, the chairman's introduction) '—is actually doing? What translations he is working on?' His voice was choked with the onset of overwhelming tears. '*He's translating nursery rhymes!* Nursery rhymes!' He looked sideways down the table, towards Smith. 'Why not give them a reading from the master's works, Ivan?' he almost screamed. 'Tell them what Goosey Goosey Gander is in—' and on that he dissolved into helpless sobs.

Nine

THE tape made a skittering squeaking noise as I re-
wound it. Then I reversed the switch, and played it
all through again, this time for pleasure.

It opened to music, as all good dramas should: an
old recording of the Don Cossack Choir singing *Occhi
Chornya*, more like a funeral dirge than a love song.
Then the technician's voice was superimposed: 'Tape
No. 642, edited. Nine p.m. May eighteenth.' Then
more droning from the Cossacks. Then suddenly
Jones's voice, clear and high:

'Oh, turn that thing off, for God's sake!'

Muffled footfalls. End of music. Smith's voice, slow
and slurring:

'What's the matter now? Changed your mind? Not
your favourite tune?'

'They sound like a lot of damned bullocks! Why
should soldiers think they can sing? You might as well

make up a choir of football players. I'm sick of music, anyway. . . . You want a drink?'

'Yes.'

Long pause. Jones's voice again: 'Pity we haven't got something to drink to.'

Smith: 'I don't imagine that will inhibit either of us.' Then more reflective: 'I wish I knew what they were trying to do to us. It would give us a line on how to react.'

'We couldn't change anything. . . . God, do you know what I was doing today?'

'Nothing, at a guess.'

'It might as well have been. I was making out lists of Foreign Service officers above the rank of First Secretary who can speak Chinese. Christ, who cares! A girl from the typing pool could have done it. Is that what we went through all that filthy business for?'

'I sometimes wonder *what* we went through it for.'

Long pause. Then Jones, rather whining, 'I can't get over that monstrous thing last night. All I wanted to do was say hallo to the man. After all, we used to know each other at home. But you'd have thought I was trying to steal his wallet!' The voice changed to mimicry. ' "*I don't know you and I don't want to know you.*" Who in hell does he think he is? A snotty little newspaper hack. But by God, I told him a thing or two. I said—'

'I heard you. . . . You know, you didn't have to throw the drink in his face. So messy. So *definite*.'

'I wish it had been a bucket of blood. Oh well, we won't go there again.'

Smith, more measured and remote: 'Perhaps we won't go anywhere again.'

'What do you mean? Drink up, Ivan. I'm miles ahead of you.'

'I mean. . . . Well, for instance, cast your eye over that mantelpiece. A year ago, you would not have been able to see it for invitations. Now—the Deputy Superintendent of Offshore Fisheries is giving a buffet supper in honour of the new Assistant Deputy, and wants us to join the company. A charming thought! I suppose we shall be fed surplus dehydrated cod. . . . And that's all we have for this week. And for next week too, by God! One might imagine that we have contracted the plague.'

Jones: 'I suppose they can't trust us not to be drunk.' Long pause. 'Oh God, this is so *dull*. . . . I think I'm hungry, after all. What about it?'

'We had better go down to the restaurant.'

'I'm sick of the restaurant. And they're always so rude.'

'Well, where else?'

'Nowhere else. . . . Let's have another before we face it.' A sound of breaking glass. 'Hell, that's one of the good glasses.'

'As long as we've got two left.'

Jones (laughs): 'That's about what it boils down to. . . . Well, cheers.'

'Have you got any money?'

'We can sign.'

A blank, a click. The technician's voice: 'Tape No. 643, edited. Eleven p.m. May eighteenth.'

Slamming door. Footsteps. Music came on again, a local radio station, and was switched off.

'I told you they'd be rude to us,' said Jones.

Smith: 'But we *were* late. Do try to be reasonable. They must have to close the kitchens some time. Waiters have to sleep.'

'They don't have to sleep on the job. And to hell with the kitchens! I want to eat my dinner in peace. And I want proper service while I'm doing it. Not to be bustled out when the clock strikes, like some wretched tourist. This damned provincial hole of a town! Oh well, we won't go there again. That's one thing sure.'

'I wish you'd stop saying that,' Smith's voice, slurring and loud with liquor like Jones's, had an impatient note. 'Your list of people and places we're never going to see again gets longer every day. What happens when we simply run out of things to boycott?'

'All I meant was—'

'All you mean is to kick up an infernal row whenever you can't get exactly what you want. Well, don't involve me in that sort of thing, because I'm sick of it. I happen to have a preference for a quiet life.'

A clink of glasses. Pause. Jones's voice: 'You might at least pour me a drink.'

'Get your own.'

'Thanks.'

'And don't break any more glasses.'

Pause. Jones's voice: 'Why the bad mood, all of a sudden?'

'It's not all of a sudden. . . . Look, Peter, this sort of life is just as boring for me as it is for you. More so, probably. But it's utterly stupid to lose your temper and stage scenes all the time. That's childish. It simply makes things worse. We've just got to put up with it. It goes with—with what we did.'

'But think of it being like this for *ever*.'

'What did you suppose it would be like?'

Long pause. Smith or Jones walking up and down, with irregular footsteps. Jones's voice again:

'We could always go back home.'

Smith: 'I very much doubt if that is true. And in any case, try and imagine what it would be like.'

'It couldn't be worse than this.'

'It could be just twice as bad! Anyway, Tollman would never let us go.'

My own nickname leapt at me out of the tape-machine loudspeaker. 'Perhaps that awful Drill-Pig man could fix it up for us.'

'He couldn't do anything of the sort. And he wouldn't try. Why on earth should he? All those Security people loathe us.'

Jones: 'How do you know? He may be just waiting for us to—' Long pause. 'Ivan, you haven't spoken to him, have you?'

'Now why in heaven's name would I do that?'

'You haven't tried—you know, to arrange something? Without telling me?'

'Of course not.'

'Then why do you say he wouldn't try? How can you know?'

'It's a matter of common-sense.'

'I'm not so sure I believe you.'

'Have it your own way.'

Jones: 'I think if something like that happened, I'd simply kill myself. We did get into this together, remember. We made that pact. We swore we'd never break it. You won't ever forget that, Ivan, will you?'

'Oh, for God's sake!'

Jones: 'Swear it. Swear it again.'

'I shall do nothing so ridiculous. Don't be so melodramatic.'

'There, you see—you won't swear.' A sound of tears in Jones's voice. 'You're not telling me the truth. You're planning to leave. I know you are.'

'Pull yourself together.'

'I can't help it. I don't know what to believe any more. We made a solemn promise that we wouldn't back out. Whatever happened. . . . This is your fault just as much as mine. In fact it was really your idea.'

Pause. Smith's voice, very cold and hard: 'That is completely untrue.'

'It's not.'

'Don't contradict me, you—you drunken little snipe! And don't tell lies. If anyone is responsible for getting us into this, it's you. And you know it. You worked on it for months. . . . Of course I was vulnerable after Patricia left me. . . . You saw that, you worked on it. If it hadn't been for you, I'd have been quite content, quite happy as things were. I would have settled down.'

'Oh God, not that again!'

'Yes, that again! You don't like to hear it because you know it's true.'

Jones: 'I suppose you're going to tell me that you were happier with her than with me.'

'Oh, don't *whine*. You sound like a child actor. . . . I never claimed to be happy with her. I loathed her. But certainly I was happier eighteen months ago than I am now. Before we came to this dreary place. . . . What do you suppose it's like for someone like myself, to live in a foreign country where I have no friends and no one to talk to, to have a stupid little job which is worse than no job at all, to have no status, no background, no social position. . . . It's the first time in my life I've felt utterly lonely, utterly cut off. . . . Good God, two years ago we had five Ambassadors to dinner, one night, and the guest of honour was Hammarskjold. Now what do we have?' There was a crash of glass; Smith must have made a sweeping gesture. 'We have nothing—nothing!'

Jones: 'We have each other.'

Smith: 'I forgot to add that to the list of drawbacks.'

Silence. Then Jones: 'I'm sorry I can't buy you all the things you're so accustomed to.'

Smith: 'What's that supposed to mean?'

'You only had them because of her. All that stuff about social position—she *bought* it for you. You know she did. You told me so, you admitted it. But you gave it up. You said it wasn't worth it. . . . If I had her money, you wouldn't be talking to me like this.'

'If I had *any* money, I wouldn't be talking to you at all.'

'You're trying to provoke me, Ivan. I know you are. Just look out, that's all. Just look out.'

'What are you going to do—throw another tantrum? Or another wine-glass? Why don't you try something original for a change?'

Jones: 'Perhaps I will.'

'One thing I will say for dear Patricia, she never threw things. . . . But you're destructive, utterly destructive. . . . You couldn't wait to talk me into this, to get me involved, to destroy everything. . . . We all have to come down to your own level, don't we? . . . Oh, for God's sake put that thing down. You look like the last act of West Side Story. . . . Now don't start that suicide nonsense again, because it doesn't impress me any longer. You haven't got the guts, even with all that drink inside you. . . . Peter, put that down. . . . Get away from me, you little hooligan! . . . Why, you must be mad! . . . I swear to God I'll—'

The voice broke off; there was only noise, confusion, thudding, then the sound of Jones's sobbing voice:

'Oh God, I'm sorry!'

Smith: 'You damned little fool, you might have killed me.'

'Oh God, I'll get some water.'

'Bathroom. . . .'

Pause, and breaks in the tape. Then quieter voices:

'Ivan.'

'Yes.'

'How does it feel now?'

'It's just a cut. I shall live.'

Jones: 'I'll make it up to you somehow, I swear I will. But don't leave me. Don't ever leave me. I can't do without you.'

'You've got a funny way of showing it, you little bastard.'

'It's only because of this place. . . . I'm just as lonely as you. . . . Ivan, what are we going to do?'

'As your rough friends would say, I suppose we're going to sweat it out.'

'But together.'

Smith, sighing: 'I'd be interested to hear what other choice we have.'

I sat for a long time in thought, after listening to the tape. I had a couple of drinks myself; I even smoked a cigar, by way of celebration. It was difficult not to gloat; it was impossible not to feel satisfied with the way things were turning out.

I could fairly say that I had foreseen the sort of development which the tape-recording had put into such crude terms. Under pressure, these people were doomed to act like this; for them, the crying jag became the murderous assault, just as surely as two and two added up to four. Smith and Jones, coming towards the end of their resources—never large, in the first place—and having no discipline to cope with disappointment, had begun to crumble. They could not hit the hated target, which was human indifference; now their only victims could be each other, and then themselves.

I could understand their despair. They had suddenly realized that they were becoming unwanted, in this new world of their choice; in reaction, they were sick for home, and it was a home which could never be theirs again. A corroding, grinding, desperate loneliness had taken the place of shortlived triumph.

Even at this stage, they could already see the end of their road, and there was no shelter, no shade, no promise of rest anywhere upon it. From now on, they must plod and trudge downhill into total dishonour. I could understand how this dark prospect was translated into drink, self-pity, suspicion, tears; into the upraised knife, the bitter remorse, and the next wave of hopelessness.

Perhaps it was truer to say that I understood it in theory. For I could not feel an ounce of pity, which for many men went with understanding. Whose fault was all this? Their own, exclusively. They had got themselves into it. They did not have to defect; they had chosen to. They had thrown away the book of rules. No one like myself would ever raise a finger to help them out.

I could never forget that I was roped and tied in the same way, and perhaps ruined in the same way.

Yet even without this, I would never have helped them. I was a policeman, and I was not going to help a man who broke the most fundamental law of this and many other centuries—the man who changed sides. Black never became white; it never even registered a shadow of grey. The award of national colours was made by chance, and by the mother who bore you. A man might not like the colour he was born to, but in this day and age he had better stick with it. Otherwise we would have to destroy him, if we could, because we were policemen. There wasn't any other reason, nor need of one. The turncoat might make other people laugh, or cry, or hate, or pity. All he did to us was to make us work. We were policemen.

There was one obvious move to be made now, by one or both of them. I was ready for it, and I had my instructions from Colonel Bellinger. They were curt instructions; in fact, they were the single word 'No'. It was only a question of how soon I would have to say it, and to which one of them; to Smith, or to Jones.

I would have bet on Jones, the erratic juvenile lead in this drama; but in fact it was Smith, the heavy, who made the approach, and it took him another two months to do so. Whether he was slow in raising the necessary courage, or whether it needed this amount of time for him to reach the saturation point of despair, I could not judge. But in the end it was he who, by devious means, got in touch with me.

For him, the means had to be devious; he was surrounded by eyes—the jealous eyes of Jones, the sharp eyes of Major Tollman. As far as I was concerned, it did not matter if Tollman knew my part in this; I had no intention of becoming really involved. But it was a matter of professional pride that, if I wanted to talk to Smith, I could do so without discovery. No Security man liked to get out of practise. In these circumstances, our meeting was not the easiest thing in the world to arrange.

Smith wrote to me, first: an ordinary letter, posted in the suburbs, which landed on my desk among a collection of bills and personal mail. It was short. He wanted to see me, without attracting any attention. He had a confidential matter to discuss. He did not think that either of us should telephone. He would leave it to me to arrange a meeting, and let him know the details, if I agreed.

It was a problem of communication, principally. I did not think that either Smith or Jones was being followed all the time, at this stage; they were hardly worth the trouble. It seemed probable that they were simply being reported on, if they said or did anything interesting in public. What I had to do, if I wanted, was to give Smith a time and a place for a safe rendezvous.

I could not be seen talking to him, at a party or anything of that sort; that really would be reported on. I might have used the girl whose favours had been rejected before; but Jones of course did not like her at all, and would have been instantly on the alert. We had a couple of waiters at the International Hotel, who could have delivered a note; however, they were not the brightest characters in the world, and were just as likely to be bluffed into giving the message to Jones as to Smith.

Finally I wrote out the exact details of what I wanted him to do. Then I sent him, by the ordinary mail, an advertisement and price-list for a firm of dry-cleaners, where we had an absolutely reliable contact; and I wrote on it: 'Special attention given to opera cloaks.' Then the dry-cleaning man called him up, and told him that they were ready to deal with his opera cloak now, as promised. Smith, who must have been waiting impatiently, caught on.

Before the cloak was returned, my message was put into one of the pockets of the lining.

I was early at the rendezvous, and strolled up and down the quay where the river tour-boats were berthed. It was the chilly, forlorn end of autumn; the massing grey clouds promised snow before many days were gone. When I went on board the boat (it was not much more than a big motor-launch) which I had chosen, it was still deserted, rocking slowly on sullen oily water. Along the river bank, lights were coming on one by one, pale in the early dusk. The season was dying; this would be one of the last boat tours of the year.

Presently Smith appeared, and stepped on board clumsily, and sat down beside me, without speaking. His breath came heavily, and sometimes, in spite of the chill, he mopped his forehead. A couple of girls on the quayside looked at us through the windows, decided we were too old and dull for profit of any kind, and made for another boat. We were still alone. A crew-man came on board, and started up the engine; then the 'captain' took his place at the wheel, and a beery old man in a yachting cap, carrying a megaphone as crinkled and battered as himself, walked down the aisle, prepared to do the honours of the capital.

He shouted: 'All aboard! Full hour's cruise!' as if we were bound for China or Peru, but it was his last show of spirit. As soon as we were under way, and he saw that we were not listening to his parrotted monotone of information, he sat down in one of the front seats, dropped his chin on his chest, and dozed off into sleep.

I turned and looked at Smith, at close quarters, for the first time in my life. Making all allowances for the strain and ordeal of the past two years, it could not be said that he was much of a sight. He had put on weight, and the shabby clothes were straining at the seams. There were food-stains on his tie. Above the gross jowls, his face was purplish, his eyes bloodshot and watery. His hands, braced on the seat in front of us, were visibly trembling. He looked like a tramp, awaiting the moment to start whining for the price of a cup of coffee. And this was the man who had marooned me in disgrace, far from home. . . . I would not have given two cents for him, dead or alive.

He did not speak for a long time; it was as if we were both using alternative senses to discover each other's thoughts. The water rippled against our bows as we glided along the nearly-deserted river; tall shadowy buildings slid by us, and were lost in the gloom astern. When we had passed under a low bridge, and the engine noise echoed hollowly against the stonework all round us, he began.

It was as I had known; he wanted to sound me out about a possible return home.

'You know why I want to see you?' was the way he started. His voice was hoarse, and he cleared his throat several times before continuing. 'This damned cold. . . . It's absolutely unbearable. . . . You've probably been waiting for something like this.'

I was not in the mood to make anything easy for him.

'I haven't been waiting at all,' I told him curtly. 'I have better things to do. . . . What's on your mind?'

Perhaps my tone discouraged him, for the tour-boat ran on for a full two minutes before he answered:

'I've been thinking things out very carefully. I made a mistake. I want to go home again.'

The 'I' struck me immediately. I wasn't going to

let him off that, either. 'Do you mean, you both feel the same way? You both want to leave?'

'Well—no.' His red-rimmed eyes wandered away from me, and stared at the lights on the embankment. 'As a matter of fact, I'm not too sure about Peter's plans. At the moment, it's just myself.'

'In fact, Jones doesn't know about this?'

He coughed noisily before answering. 'We haven't really discussed it.'

We passed under another bridge, and out into more open water. The old man in the yachting cap stirred, opened his eyes, and looked towards us; he raised his megaphone, and called out: 'This is the widest point of the river, within the city limits. It is accustomed to remain open until February. In 1925, and again in 1937, it did not freeze over at all.' Then he subsided once more. A ghostly building, faceless, like a grain elevator, came into view on the far bank. The boat sounded a mournful note on its whistle: then it began a wide sweep, turning for home.

Smith said: 'What are the prospects?'

'There are no prospects,' I answered.

It was a pleasure to watch him as he turned towards me, his fat face stricken. 'You can't mean it!' He was almost stammering. 'Why not?'

'Because we don't want you back.'

'But that doesn't *begin* to make sense! You *must* want me back! Think of how it could be presented. Think of its value as a story. I was so disillusioned, so disgusted with the life here—'

'Who cares what you think of the life here?'

'But there are *millions* of people—'

His voice died under my gaze. 'The story is worth nothing,' I told him. 'Because you are worth nothing. Not as a witness, not as a man. You changed over once. Now you want to change over again. Who wants people like that? Who wants a traitor who can't even make up his mind?'

The key word had hit him hard; he could not deal with it. 'They don't really want us here, either,' he muttered. 'Only for show. . . . How were we to know it would be over so quickly?'

'You should have thought of that before.' I had waited a long time to say this; it came out rough and strong, the way I had often thought of it. 'You'd better face it, Smith. Nobody wants you. Not here, not at home. Especially not the influential people who are sending money to Jones every month. They're paying him to stay away and keep quiet. Why don't you get someone to pay you?'

He made an effort at dignity. 'I know nothing of that. . . . It doesn't concern me. . . .' He fell into silence again, for a long time. Then he said: 'I don't understand. If you were going to refuse, why did you agree to meet me? Why go through with such a farce'?

'I wanted to see what you looked like.'

'And?'

'Now I'm even less likely to say yes.'

We were edging towards the shore; the throb of the engine died away to a faint pulse. The old man began to stir himself, bleary and stiff, licking dry lips, needing his drink. The brave voyage was over.

'What's to become of us?' asked Smith hopelessly. It was 'us' again, now. 'What can we do?'

I almost answered 'Sweat it out', but caution intervened. 'Live with it,' I answered.

'It's no life.' He put his hand on my arm; it brought an instant revulsion, and I shook it off. He said humbly: 'Won't you please reconsider?'

I did not answer. I had had my revenge, or some of it. It was not as great a moment as I had hoped, but it would do for now. The boat bumped and scraped against the dockside, and the old man called out 'Come again' as we stepped ashore. Smith shambled off ahead of me, moving from lamp to lamp down the length of the quay. Till he was out of sight in the gloom, I waited, sniffing the cold air, and the river smells, and the first small triumph of a long siege.

But it turned out that, professionally, I had not done so well; and Smith had not done so well either. The river dusk had sprouted more eyes than I had thought possible. I had two telephone calls, that same night, which demonstrated this beyond doubt.

The first was from Major Tollman. He was not at all affable, not at all unofficial; now he was a Security shark with its teeth showing, which was something one rarely met. He started without preamble:

'I hope you're not going to disappoint me.'

I had not been expecting the call; but it was easy to

guess what it was about, and easier still to pay Tollman the compliment of not hedging.

'No,' I answered, 'I'm not going to disappoint
you.'

I thought that the slight emphasis would be enough
for him; but he had questions to ask, and things to
say, and it became clear that he did not intend to let
me go until he had spelled it all out.

'Why the meeting, then?' he asked curtly.

I gave the same, the almost-true answer I had
given Smith. 'I wanted to see what he looked like.
Close to.'

'We can tell you what he looks like, any time. You
don't have to make a personal inspection.' His voice
took on a sharper edge. 'I strongly advise you to tell
me what this is all about.'

'Major, you're making too much out of this.' Since
my conscience was clear, I felt that I could sound a
reasonably firm note. 'Our friend and I talked for an
hour or so. You can guess what it was about, if you
haven't done so already. The answer was "No".'

'His answer?'

'No. My answer.'

There was silence on the telephone, while he
worked this out and, I hoped, shed a few suspicions.
But, having struck a certain attitude, he was not yet
ready to abandon it. His voice came back, harsh and
grim.

'I don't like the sound of this at all. And I warned
you what would happen if I started not to like it. I

tell you frankly—if you've been trying to get at our friend, there's going to be hell to pay.'

'I have not been trying to get at our friend. Who wants our friend? Apart from *his* friend. We're perfectly happy with things as they are.'

There was another silence, a disbelieving one. Then Tollman tried something else.

'Have they quarrelled? Is that what it is?'

'Not more than usual.'

'Don't fool with me,' he snapped. 'I'm not in the mood. If he came to see you on his own account, they've quarrelled. If he was speaking for both of them, then they haven't quarrelled. Which was it?'

I thought that over quickly. There seemed no point in giving aid and comfort to the enemy. In fact there was no point in giving anything; I did not have to help Tollman with his homework, or anyone else. 'The whole thing was exploratory,' I said. 'A simple little trial balloon. They just don't like it here.' I decided to make a point of my own. 'Can you blame them?'

'I'm not sure who to blame,' he countered. 'But I'll find out. . . . Do *you* like it here?'

'Enough,' I said. 'Cooking is not your national strong point. But otherwise. . . .'

'I'm telling you again,' he barked out, 'don't fool with this! If you like it here, keep quiet and we'll put up with you. If you're trying to start something, you won't last twenty-four hours.'

I decided that I had gone far enough. 'Major, I like it here.'

'All right.' His voice was receding, as if he were dropping the telephone and the subject at the same time. 'I'll take your word for it, until I find out to the contrary. But I'm warning you—don't get on my list.'

With the easing of tension, I eased my own. 'Is that a long list, Major?'

'No,' he said. There was, at last, a ghost of humour in his voice. 'It never gets very long. Somehow, I always manage to lop off the names at the top.' And with that, he was gone.

Not more than an hour later, the telephone rang again. With twenty guesses, I could not have named the caller in advance. It was Jones. He was drunk, but, like many a seasoned drunkard, he was explicit and articulate, for all that. He started on a crude note of insult.

'Is that the Drill-Pig?'

I had not heard the nickname spoken to me, in my own or any other language, for a long time. On my guard, and still pondering the call from Major Tollman, I answered warily:

'Who's that?'

'You know perfectly well who it is.' Jones's voice, which I had recognized straight away, was shrill and strangled; the soft babyish harmonies had given place to something quite different. 'Drill-Pig,' he said, 'I've one question to ask you.'

I would have hung up, but this was a question I had to hear. So I waited.

Against a background of music, Jones asked: 'What did Ivan say to you?'

The only thing to do with this was to enjoy it.

'It was a confidential matter,' I answered. 'I don't think I can tell you about it.'

'Is he trying to go home?'

'I really don't know what you're talking about.'

There was a sob at the other end of the telephone. 'Oh God!' said Jones. 'How can people be so cruel? . . . Why are you all such brutes? . . . You've *got* to tell me. . . . Tell me what you two talked about. . . . I absolutely demand to know. . . . Did he mention going home?'

'It did come up,' I answered.

'Together?' The voice rose to a sudden wild scream. 'He asked for both of us?'

Suddenly I had had enough of this topic and these people; I was sick of the whole nest of snakes.

'Your friend,' I said, 'is a selfish man. He wasn't inquiring about a group trip.'

'That's all I want to know,' said Jones, and on a choking sound the telephone went blank again.

Ten

THE death of Smith, sensational and macabre, made a fantastic public impression. As a newsworthy couple, they had very nearly dropped out of sight; their story had withered and died, in favour of dozens of other stories, long before Smith and Jones themselves had realized it. But now they had bounced back, in a single stroke which revived the whole thing again; now suddenly they returned to the headlines, and the headlines were screaming.

All the way round the world, a lot of different things were taken for granted, as soon as the news broke; massive political libels were committed in every second paragraph; as had happened over the original defection, sides were chosen before the actual event. Half the world took it for granted that we had murdered Smith out of revenge; the other half proclaimed that he had died of sheer boredom in an utterly boring society.

'BLOOD ON THE SNOW!' shouted one of the New York tabloids, less than accurately. The death of Smith had no blood about it. But it had almost everything else.

Smith was discovered, early one winter morning, frozen to death in one of the city's main parks. He had been there all night, as far as could be established; the temperature, in the first big drop of the winter, had gone down to fifteen below zero; having no over-coat, he could hardly have survived more than a few hours. He had a broken ankle, the result (it seemed) of having slipped and fallen on an icy pathway. But he was a strong man, and he might have dragged himself to safety and warmth, on one of the lighted city streets a hundred yards away, if he had been free to move.

He was not free to move, because he had been handcuffed to a tree.

In all the newspaper accounts, a large amount of space was devoted to Jones. For Jones had disappeared at the same time, and people were invited to draw their own conclusions, according to their political colour. He could be a murderer on the run, or he could be in deadly danger himself. 'Some fears are entertained for his safety,' was how *The Times* of London put it. 'GUESS WHO'S NEXT?' was the crisper version in the *Daily Mirror*.

The papers also made a lot of play with the handcuffs, and one had to admit that they gave the death of Smith an odd aura of officialdom. Policemen used handcuffs; therefore . . . . But it was the handcuffs which were, for me, the essential clue to what had actually happened. Jones had a pair of handcuffs. He had worn them, to complete his squalid masquerade as a slave girl, at the costume party just after the two of them defected. I even knew where he had bought them—at Jolly Jack's Joke Shop (Magicians' Supplies) on the main shopping street of the capital. But they were real handcuffs—or at least they were a good enough joke to chain a big man to a tree all night.

Jones had killed Smith—I had no doubt of that. From what I knew, from all the facts on the file, I could reconstruct the how and the why.

Smith and Jones had kept very quiet since the boat trip, and the telephone call to myself afterwards. I had been expecting some sort of explosion, but nothing happened; they had settled down in an atmosphere of uneventful domestic bliss which I knew now to be false. Jones, a loving yet vindictive person, had not forgiven Smith for making the treacherous approach to me; he had simply been biding his time. Having planned exactly how to take his revenge, he had been waiting for the first bitter cold of winter to do it.

It all fell neatly into place. Smith and Jones had gone for a late evening walk together, in the deserted, ill-lit park not far from the International Hotel. Smith had slipped on the sloping pathway, or more probably had been pushed from behind, and had broken his ankle. Jones had been ready to knock him unconscious, but this had not been necessary; the fall itself, and the pain of the fracture, had put Smith out. Jones had wrestled him out of his overcoat (or had cut it off the inert body), dragged his victim to the nearest small tree, handcuffed his arms round the trunk, said goodbye, and walked away whistling.

The minus 15 degree temperature—the thing Jones had been waiting for—had done the rest.

Now Jones had gone into hiding—somewhere in this sprawling, untidy city where it was so easy to hide. I guessed that he would come out, sooner or later, and claim that he had escaped an attempt at double murder, and had subsequently been holed up, in fear of his life. He was probably waiting to see how the news was interpreted. But whatever happened, he would doubtless give a moving performance as a man, stricken by sorrow at the loss of a beloved friend, emerging in grief and terror to claim the just protection of the law.

At least, that was what I thought, until Ambassador Black and Colonel Bellinger together gave me quite a different idea, and quite a different problem.

It was the week-end, a hallowed pause in this and many other parts of the world. Business died its weekly death, diplomacy took a holiday; offices were closed, telephones went unanswered, doctors and lawyers could not be reached, except possibly at the

Country Club; the world went fishing—or, in this particular climate, skiing, curling, skating, and drinking. Our Embassy was closed, save for the cypher staff standing their watch in the basement; the building, when I entered with my pass-key, was silent, and my footsteps echoed down long empty corridors and hallways. In Ambassador Black's study, where I joined him and Blaustein, even our voices had a hollow ring, as if we were men talking on a bare mountain side. For all the good we were doing, I thought, that might well have been the case.

Ambassador Black was ill-at-ease and nervous; a reporter had tried to waylay him on the doorstep, and he had not appreciated the attempt. Blaustein, a small, sharp-eyed man, looked as if he were trying not to be there at all; at this moment, he was not in the least ambitious to take over my job—or to take over any job; he was well content that bigger men with bigger labels should shoulder this load of trouble.

It was I who was in the spotlight again; the Smith and Jones assignment—*my* assignment—had taken a truly sour turn, and all that these men wanted to do was to give it a decisive shove in my direction.

Ambassador Black was almost peevish, as he reviewed the death of Smith. 'They think *we* did it,' he said, glaring at me as if this could only be my fault. 'They actually think we had him murdered, to pay him back for defecting!'

'Who is "they"?' I asked.

'Everybody.' He gave a nervous jerk to his shoulders. 'You've seen the papers, you must have heard the talk. . . . It's too ridiculous! We just don't do that sort of thing. If anyone did it, for political motives, *they* did it.'

I forebore to ask which particular 'they' this was. Instead I said:

'I don't agree with you. I'm almost sure that Jones did it.'

'Jones?' Ambassador Black's little blue eyes settled on me with a frosty snap. 'I would doubt that. I would seriously doubt that. . . . What evidence is there?'

I told him about the handcuffs, while he continued his disbelieving stare, and Blaustein puffed away at a cigarette as if this were all he could legitimately be called upon to do. 'It's the old story,' I concluded. 'Smith tried to leave him. Love turned to hate. Jones was waiting for revenge, and now he's taken it.'

Ambassador Black made a grimace. 'Honestly, the kind of people you send us nowadays. . . . Love turned to hate. . . . Good God!' He continued to look as if we were discussing my favourite sort of person, and that only he stood between the Foreign Service and a degrading chaos. 'I don't agree. I think *they* did it, because—' he waved his hand, 'oh, all sorts of things. Principally, so that it would look as if *we* did it. It's made a thoroughly bad impression, anyway. It looks like a revenge killing. All this publicity. . . . And there might be worse to come.'

Blaustein gazed at his cigarette, intently; it was I who had to ask the question, to show the strength of my engagement. 'What sort of thing?'

'Jones,' answered Ambassador Black. 'Where is he? What happens if he is found dead? We could be in real trouble. . . . You know what people will say? We had them *both* killed! Where will we be then?'

'It still doesn't lead to us.'

'Of course it leads to us! People add these things up, you know. Two and two make four. We've got to be very careful. This is a real hot one.'

'What would you suggest?'

'Firstly, we've got to keep quiet. No statements, no comments of any kind.' I wondered who was likely to make a statement; once again, it seemed to be myself. 'Then, we've got to find Jones.' His eyes sharpened. '*You've* got to find Jones. Wherever he is. Whatever he has or hasn't done. You've got to find him, and make sure he stays alive, before anything else happens.'

'I still don't see what could happen,' I objected. 'My theory is that he's hiding, until he sees which way the wind is blowing. In fact, I'm quite sure of it. Then he'll come out, and start bluffing his way out of trouble. We don't have to keep him alive.'

'I'm not interested in your theory,' said Ambassador Black. 'Matter of fact, I think it's a lot of nonsense. So let's take it from there. . . . This is an obvious frame-up. We're being framed for one murder. We may still be framed for two, to make it even more convincing. You've got to put a stop to that. You've got to find Jones, and make sure nothing happens to him.'

He stood up, suddenly; the pushing back of his chair made a hollow scraping sound on the parquet floor, which seemed to echo all over the empty building. The interview was over, and he was walking away from any argument. I had my orders; once again, this was my problem, and its solving was my responsibility, and I needn't come back until I had the answer. 'You've got to find Jones,' repeated Ambassador Black, by way of farewell; and this was all the help and all the comfort I had, as I made my way down the wide staircase, and prepared to step out into a very cold world.

But before I stepped out, I had another prod from higher up; another directive which, while it made my assignment seem less silly, did not make it less crucial. When I reached the main entrance hall, I heard my name called, and a man came up the stairs from the basement nest of vaults, safes, coding rooms, and radio equipment which was a significant part of the Embassy. He was a cypher officer, one of our own men whom I knew personally; and he tendered a pink envelope with the appropriate air of importance.

'Heard you were here, sir,' he said. 'Top Secret, personal to you.' And he added, in the customary cypher-staff jargon: 'May I have your autograph?'

I signed the printed release-form clipped to the

envelope, and handed it over. When he had gone back to his lair, I slit the envelope and took out the cable. It was from Colonel Bellinger, and, as a good example of Bellinger in action, Bellinger glaring across his desk in cold print, it is worth quoting in full.

'TOP SECRET,' it began. 'Personal to Third Secretary Special Duties from Bellinger SECARM. BEGINS:

'PARA ONE. Death of Smith is severe propaganda setback which must NOT repeat NOT be allowed to deteriorate. Your lack of surveillance despite explicit instructions to the contrary has led to death which can be attributed to one of three following causes:

(1) Official murder by host country.

(2) Revenge murder by Jones.

(3) Murder by Jones prompted by bribe from host country.

'PARA TWO. I incline to (2) above, but in any case propaganda value of death works to our definite disadvantage.

'PARA THREE. Probable next development will be one of following:

(1) Jones will now be killed to complete pattern of execution which can be attributed to us.

(2) Jones will commit suicide in circumstances which further involve us in complicity.

'PARA FOUR. It is of paramount importance that Jones remain alive. At all costs repeat at all costs you should find Jones, dissuade him from further action, take him under protection if necessary, and arrange repatriation if so desired. It is your personal responsibility, and an essential part of your mission, to produce Jones in good health at press conference or similar public inspection. You have free hand, unlimited funds, and authority to give him any undertaking regarding his future.

'PARA FIVE. I must emphasize that failure will have serious international consequences and cannot be tolerated. ENDS.'

'Find Jones' seemed to be the popular slogan. Everyone was using it, everyone had the same idea, from fools like Ambassador Black to office martinets like Colonel Bellinger. It turned out that even Major Tollman, who was neither of these things, had the same idea too.

I had to go to a routine diplomatic reception, that Saturday evening. It was a dull affair, not enlivened by the fact that Smith and Jones seemed to be the sole topic of conversation. But there, in one corner, was Major Tollman; withdrawn from common circulation, watching instead of talking, yet seeming to enjoy himself. On an impulse, I took a strengthening whisky and soda from the buffet table, and made my way over to him.

'Good evening, Major.'

He had been observing me as I made my approach, and was ready for the encounter. 'Mr. Third Secretary,' he said, affably. 'I didn't expect to see you. I would have thought you were too busy tonight, to have any spare time for this sort of thing.'

'A short pause,' I answered. 'After all, it *is* the week-end. Things come to a stop.'

'A British habit, surely. Not for you. Not for us. Not for Mr. Jones.' He smiled, quite pleasantly, as if he were making the kind of joke which sharks, at least, found funny. 'I think we can say that for Mr. Smith, things have come to a stop. A dead stop.'

'Sad, but true.'

'Sad?' His eyes sharpened suddenly; he was looking at me as if he really wanted to find something out. 'I thought perhaps that I should congratulate you.'

'On what?'

'On squaring accounts.' His manner was now almost jovial. 'And perhaps on saving us some trouble.'

'We didn't do it,' I said. I found that I could not react to his tone. I was not jovial, or anything like it; as I sniffed the confines of the tightest corner of my life, all men were my enemies. 'Or, if you mean me personally, I didn't do it. I'm sure you know that's true.'

'Is it?' He was still watching me carefully. 'Well, now. . . . I must tell you that we very nearly asked you to come down and talk to us.'

'Why? I had nothing to do with it.'

'Possibly. Possibly not. But in any case the effect on public opinion might have been worthwhile. People have this unfortunate weakness for believing that anyone interviewed by the police must be guilty. However, we decided that there would be too many protocol complications.' Then he waved his hand, as if disposing of the topic; and frankly, I was very glad of it. I had enough troubles already, without being accused of a murder which had dictated perhaps the worst turn of my career. Major Tollman took a sip of a drink which looked like vodka, but which I suspected was iced water. 'I detect,' he said, more gently, 'a certain preoccupation tonight. Are they riding you hard?'

Once again, it seemed that this man was more my friend than many other people on my own side. 'Pretty hard,' I said. 'I didn't foresee any of this.'

He nodded. 'And your Ambassador? His Excellency Mr. Black? How does he think Smith died?'

It was a time for frankness. 'He thinks you did it.'

'What do you think?'

'I think Jones did it. But we shall be blamed, anyway.'

'Not in the long run. Not if you find Jones.'

'That's not too easy.'

Major Tollman set down his empty glass. 'I agree. I may say that we are also looking for him.'

'Why?'

'Because, contrary to the popular belief in your country, we don't like murderers.' Now he was glancing about him; he either wanted to talk to someone else, or he was leaving the party. In either case he was leaving me, and I felt the more lonely for it. 'You should find Jones,' he said, out of the side of his mouth. 'I can give you all sorts of reasons, but the real one is the best. Because it's your job. . . . Find him. Neutralize him. Take him home, for all we care. . . . We have had—what is the expression those horrible sports-writers use?—we have had enough mileage out of Mr. Jones. He and Smith were *very* useful to us, when they first arrived. Now they are not. They poison the air for honest men.' His eyes swung round to me suddenly. 'I mean, for the honest men in this country who hate your country.' He smiled, a baleful shark at the top of his profession. 'Make no mistake—we would be glad to see you all in hell. We propose to do so, in our own good time. But we prefer to choose our allies, and our weapons. . . . Find Jones,' he concluded. 'I can assure you, we won't grudge you the prize.'

Find Jones. I went to bed with the thought, and dreamed uneasily of pursuit and capture, and woke to a Sunday morning on which Jones had still to be found. I did not know how. He might be anywhere. This was not the biggest city in the world, and by now I knew it well; but any city was big enough to hide a man. Only in quiet villages was a stranger obtrusive; in towns and cities, he disappeared into a faceless crowd, he could hole up in one of a thousand attics, hotel rooms, boarding-houses, charity lodgings. Or he found a friend, and lay hid in comfort and security.

He disappeared, and who would know where to look first?

Find Jones. Everyone had the same idea. Presently it turned out that Jones had it himself—Jones, the only man in the world who could make it easy for me. While I was getting breakfast, he telephoned.

'Is that the Drill-Pig?' His voice was faint, as if he were tired, or half asleep, or thinking of something else. 'I want to see you, Drill-Pig.'

I might still have been dreaming, the kind of absurd dream which, even while you are dreaming it, you know cannot be true. I was not sure how to answer this astonishing call. I smelt a trap of some sort, the outline of a frame-up, the first hint of treacherous malice, and it seemed important to gauge his mood. So I said:

'I'm not so sure I want to see you. What's been going on? Where are you?'

'You know what's been going on.' The voice, though still faint, had overtones of sneering self-confidence. 'Perhaps you don't know why I want to see you. But you're looking for me, aren't you?'

'A lot of people are looking for you.'

'But the Drill-Pig most of all. You're in trouble, Drill-Pig, and you know it. You haven't a prayer. . . . You'd better do as I say.'

'Perhaps we ought to have a talk,' I answered, as calmly as I could. I was none the wiser as to why he had called, but there was one crucial fact, which dictated all that I did: trap or not, frame-up or not, I

could not afford to lose touch with him. I asked again:
'Where are you?'

The answer, mocking, far away, was the worst one
I could have imagined:

'I'm in your office.'

Eleven

WHEN the phone went dead, and I put it down again, all the complications that might come from Jones being inside our Embassy hit me with stunning force. It was something I had never foreseen, because I believed it to be impossible; the fact that it had happened started a train of confusion and fear which wrecked all normal thoughts and feelings.

I abandoned breakfast, and dressed as quickly as I could; I even had a drink, a stiff shot of brandy which any drinking man would have recognized as the morning nerve-quencher. Then, because I did not want to believe the facts, and had turned to wondering how they could be true, I called Ambassador Black. I had a theory, or rather a discomforting guess at what might have happened, and this seemed the quickest way to check its validity.

Ambassador Black sounded as if he were still in

bed; he also sounded bad-tempered, and ready to demonstrate that half-past nine on a Sunday morning was no time to telephone an Ambassador, even for the most cogent reasons. But since I gave no reasons of any sort, he did not have much ammunition; and I put my questions, and extracted the answers, with very little opposition.

'When Smith and Jones defected,' I began, 'what happened to their keys?'

'Keys?' said the Ambassador grumpily. 'What on earth are you talking about? What keys? What do you want to know for, anyway?'

'I'm just checking a theory,' I answered. 'I mean their official keys. What was done about them?'

'We changed all the locks, naturally.' His voice grew querulous. 'You don't imagine Smith and Jones turned in their keys before they took off, do you? They kept the keys, or threw them away, so we altered the locks. As a matter of routine. It was the only thing to do.'

'You changed all the locks?'

'All the ones that mattered. The safe—well, only Smith had a key to that. The registry. Their own offices. Things like that.'

'What about the Embassy itself? The front door?'

'We didn't change that one. Why should we? There's always a guard there, or a caretaker. No one can get past the front hall, anyway.'

'What about the other door? The garden door the staff use in the summer?'

'Well—' he hesitated, 'well—no. There was no point in going to extremes. The internal keys were the ones that mattered. No one's going to climb into the garden, and try to—' he realized that he assumed the defensive, and he didn't like it, so he checked himself. 'Look here,' he said irritably, 'what *is* this? You'd better tell me before we go any further.'

But I didn't tell him. I said: 'It's a theory, and I'm satisfied,' and rang off. I didn't tell him for many reasons; partly because he was such a useless ally, chiefly because I had been angry at the way I had been treated, for a very long time, and had grown determined in my isolation. Solve the Smith and Jones affair, I had been told, repeatedly; it is yours. Very well, then, I now thought; it was mine, and I would solve it.

But it was enough to know that Jones had spoken the truth, and that he had got into my office in the Embassy, to renew all fears and doubts, and to begin to lose hope, even before I came face to face with the job itself.

Through empty Sunday morning streets, through trodden snow and the crisp rime of ice, through bright sunshine, I walked the half mile to the Embassy. I had plenty to think about, but I could not make my thoughts add up to anything. I was still guessing; the only thing certain was a sense of foreboding, a conviction that things had taken a bad turn for me, and that Jones would, if he could, make them worse. As I walked past houses where the sun melted icicles from the eaves, as I trudged the river bank with the frozen river on my right-hand gleaming like a huge frosted mirror, my thoughts whirled around a dozen possibilities.

I did not have a gun (it was locked in my office safe, to appease local sensitivities), nor any means of taking Jones prisoner. I was stronger than he, and could have overpowered him without difficulty; but he was doubtless armed himself, he would never let me get near him. . . . I still did not know what he wanted. If he planned to give himself up, he would not have done it like this. If he were seeking asylum for the second time, he would never have taunted me with having got into my office; he would have been polite, even humble. . . . He had said, on the telephone: 'You'd better do as I say'; therefore he knew he had the whip-hand, and he aimed somehow to use it.

If anything happened in the Embassy, anything scandalous or violent, anything which brought the police or attracted a crowd, I might well be ruined.

Well, I was there, anyway.

I let myself in by the Embassy front door. The week-end caretaker, a sulky old man with a limp, stumped out into the hall as he heard the door close, and stood looking at me. 'I'm going up to my office,' I said, and stepped past him across the mosaic-tiled floor. He did not answer, but turned and went limping back to his cubby-hole, his chair, his pipe and paper. He was the caretaker. He did not have to like people. Even the people who paid his wages.

In the hollow, echoing silence, I began to climb the stairs to my room. There were three flights, and they grew meaner as they rose to unfashionable levels; first there was marble and pile carpet, then pegged teak and terylene rug, then pine boards and strips of linoleum. At the top floor, I made my way along the corridor to my office, and tried the door. It was, as I expected, bolted from the inside. I knocked, and after a pause Jones's voice said:

'Who is it?'

I spoke my name, as quietly as I could.

'Give the password,' said Jones.

'What is it?'

'Drill-Pig.'

I had no choice in this stupid by-play. 'Drill-Pig,' I repeated.

'Correct,' said the voice. There was a pause, then the sound of steps on the other side of the door. Jones spoke again:

'I'm going to unlock the door. Don't open it until I say so. In fact, you can knock again, before you come in.' There was a sudden metallic click, almost beside my ear. 'Recognize that noise?'

I said 'No,' though I had done so.

'Revolver,' said Jones. 'Very old-fashioned forty-five. Makes a hole at least six inches wide in anybody's stupid head. Just remember.'

He pulled back the bolt, and retreated, and after a moment I knocked again.

'Come in,' said Jones. 'Very slowly. *Suaviter in modo*, like the man used to say.' When I was inside, he said: 'Shut the door. Bolt it, without turning round. Then stop where you are.'

After I had obeyed, Jones gave an unexpected giggle, and said: 'Advance, Drill-Pig, and be recognized. Isn't that what those silly soldiers say? Advance Drill-Pig. But don't advance too far.'

I came forward. Jones was sitting at my desk, leaning back in my chair, and levelling the revolver straight at my head. He looked terrible; worse than I had ever seen him, worse than on the morning in Belgrade when he had come straight from a night in prison. He was rumpled and unshaven; his face was almost transparent with fatigue; by contrast, the shadows under his eyes were nearly black. Yet his manner was still jaunty; the bottle of whisky—my whisky—on the desk was less than half full; he had been getting his courage and, I suppose, his endurance from a traditional source. Even as I watched, he picked up the bottle with his free hand, and took a gurgling swig of raw liquor, defiantly, like a schoolboy breaking the most sacred of rules, and then set the bottle down again with a crash.

I had the impression that he was less drunk than he advertised; that he was almost hypnotizing himself into drunkenness, as if he needed to manufacture a fortified Peter Jones in order to cope with some desperate act. He was wishing that the whisky were stronger, so that he himself might be stronger. . . .

When he saw me examining him in this clinical fashion, he suddenly snapped:

'Don't stare at me, damn you! I'm not in your kindergarten any longer.' He leant sideways; the revolver wavered uncertainly, then levelled off again, dead in line with my chest. 'Sit down, Drill-Pig. Sit there, where I can see you.' When I had sat down, as directed, on the hard chair on the opposite side of the desk, he said: 'Now we'll call the meeting to order.'

I waited, not even wondering what I should do; in this room, with this man, in face of the aimed gun, I was not much more than a dummy figure. I glanced idly round the office, where I had spent hours and days and months in frustrating hack-work, filling in the time, waiting for this very man to do something, make some mistake, show some weakness. Now we had reached the end of that wearying road, and I was still waiting: but the choice was still his, and the guesswork still mine.

When I looked at Jones once more, he was playing with a pencil on the desk, flipping it up a small slope of newspaper, waiting for it to come rolling back again. He had laid down the revolver, though its muzzle was still towards me and his hand was close beside it. Stillness reigned; whatever he had in mind, he was not yet ready for it. Presently the pencil fell to the floor, with a rattling sound; and Jones, in a small dispirited voice, said:

'Make some light conversation, Drill-Pig.' When

I was still silent, he added sharply: 'Don't you want to know *anything*?'

There were so many things I wanted to know, and the occasion was so odd, that I suddenly felt impelled to make the most of it. At the back of my mind was the secondary idea, that if he were kept talking long enough, he might lose his watchfulness, or even fall asleep. But for one or other of us, for Jones or for me, this must assuredly be our last appearance on any significant stage. Without special effort, I posed the first important question that came into my mind.

'All right,' I said. 'Tell me why you defected.'

Jones came to life with an ugly cackling laugh. 'I knew you'd ask that! You people really are the limit! Tell *me* something—what's it like, being so awful?'

'Am I awful?'

Jones nodded vigorously. 'Grisly! Quite monstrous! You just never stop. Run, run, run, as long as there's anything moving in sight. I'd rather starve than have that kind of job! Or that kind of mentality.'

'You haven't answered my question.'

'I defected,' said Jones snappishly, 'to get away from people like you.'

I said, off-hand: 'That's not a worthwhile answer. But perhaps it doesn't matter.'

Jones reacted to my tone, as I knew he would; even in this lunatic situation, he still needed to be the focus of interest, he had to have his audience. 'You really want to know?' he asked.

'Yes.'

He took a drink, a smaller one, and this time laid the bottle down gently. Then he put his chin on one hand, and looked at me. 'I'll tell you,' he said, 'because it *is* important. Whether it will mean anything to you, I couldn't begin to guess. And I couldn't care less.'

After that, he was silent for a long minute; then suddenly he began to talk, readily and articulately, as if he were glad of the chance; as if he had a lot to say, and had not been able to say it to a new person for a long time. There was no need to prompt him now; he took off, in full flight, on the quest for justification.

'It's two separate stories, of course.' he began. 'Ivan and I were always madly different. We had the same idea about coming here, but nothing like the same reasons. With Ivan, it was much more an emotional decision; he was fed up, that terrible woman was giving him hell, he had to break away or he would have gone absolutely mad. Patricia destroyed him, of course. And then he destroyed himself, all over again. He made up his mind that he had to keep moving on, for life to be tolerable.' Jones paused for a brooding moment. 'You know he was trying to leave me. After all I'd done for him, after all the sacrifices I'd made. But I did the leaving. I left him! I just chained him up and walked away!'

He paused, as if he awaited a comment, and I said: 'That wasn't much of a death.'

'Ivan had to be punished,' said Jones. 'I don't

expect people like you to understand these things. . . . Well, anyway, that was his reason for coming here—Patricia, and everything that went with her. I told you it was purely emotional. For me, it was quite different.'

He refreshed himself, deliberately, from the whisky bottle; this was to be the big speech, the Jones scene; he wanted to do it perfectly.

'I had *real* reasons for coming here,' he said. 'Frankly, I just can't stand our country. It has everything wrong with it—everything! Smug. Self-satisfied. Narrow-minded. Conformist. Mad about power and prestige, not caring a damn about the real things. And everyone has to fit in! Unless you stay in your appointed niche and behave like a good boy from the cradle to the grave, you might as well be dead. And it's absolutely brutal to the artist! I can prove it from my own experience!'

He leant forward across the desk, and began to speak faster. 'I am a poet,' he said. 'I've written some *beautiful* poetry. When I used to read it at parties, people cried! I actually saw them crying! But what can a poet do, in our sort of society? I'll tell you. He can starve. That's all he can do. Do you think I could make a living as a poet? Do you think I could even get my poems published?' He gestured wildly. 'I had to stop writing, and take that ridiculous cultural job, just to stay alive! As if you can sell culture by the pound to anyone that comes along! But it was the only thing to do. I tell you, I was desperate. That's what my wonderful country does to its poets and writers and artists! It puts them in an office, and tells them to work a forty-hour week at something useful and productive and sensible, and never, never, *never* say anything that might upset people. Especially Drill-Pig people like you.'

He paused, to recover his breath; and, with nothing to lose, I put in an oblique word for our side.

'There might have been all sorts of reasons why you couldn't get your poems published.'

'There was only one reason,' he declared with angry emphasis. 'It was the reason they gave, damn them! They said my writing was just experimental. *Just* experimental! As if experimenting was easy to do! Or as if there was something immoral about it! How can we go anywhere without experiment? I thought our country was *the* experimental country. Always ready to try anything, always ready for new ideas. Perhaps it is. But not poetry! New bombs. New rockets. New cars. New kinds of bread. New soap-flakes. New synthetic clothes for new synthetic people. But poetry? Good God! Run that subversive swine out of town!'

He broke off again; he really was becoming exhausted, and though I could not yet see how to turn it to advantage, at least talking was better than action, the words so far had maintained precedence over the gun. All I wanted to do at the moment was to keep him at it. When his breathing grew more quiet, I asked:

'Did you try to have your poems published here?'

'Who could possibly translate them?' Jones gave me a disdainful look. 'That's not the point, anyway,' he said, pettishly. 'I'm talking about what happened at home, and why I came here. I *hated* my country for what it did to me. And for everything else that's so wrong with it. I still hate it.' He gave me another look, different, more appraising; a look of steady calculation. 'I really think I would do any damage to it, that I could. And I would do any damage to you, too, for the same reason. But that's something we'll come to, before very long.'

I saw then that there was, after all, not a great deal of hope in this situation. Jones was not going to forget, nor was he going to fall asleep; he was going to talk enough to justify himself, drink enough to climax his courage, taunt me enough to satisfy his hatred, and then—and then, I did not know what. But after ten or fifteen minutes, I was no nearer to getting control of this crisis than I had been when I first knocked on the door. I was still the dummy figure, the wax image that other people did things to. I did not know what Jones was going to do to me. I could only guess that it must be worth delaying, at any cost. With an effort, I put another question, or rather I said something which I hoped would spark him again.

'Facts are facts,' I said bluntly. 'You may not like us any more, you may even have had a raw deal, but you can't wave the facts away, you can't eat them, or spit them out. You happen to have been born in one particular half of the world. No matter what you think of it now, you still owe it your loyalty, for as long as you live. You just can't escape that.'

'Spoken like a true policeman,' said Jones tartly. 'Anyway, you're quite wrong. I did escape it.'

I shook my head. 'You never did.'

After a moment, he said: 'No—in a way, I never did. But I'm going to.'

I disregarded this last sentence; it was not the topic I wanted. 'You never did,' I pressed him, 'because it wasn't any better when you came here. Was it? Be honest. What was it really like?'

'It was *great* fun,' said Jones, in a skittish way which I found revolting. Then he switched, on the instant, to something more serious. 'It really was fun, to start with. You've heard of the life of Riley? This was the life of Smith and Jones. We had an absolutely fantastic time, for about six months. I suppose that was the calculated period of reward. After that— well, let's say that our privileges were withdrawn.'

'How do you mean?'

'They murdered us,' said Jones simply. 'They took us by the *ego* and screwed the life out of us. You would have been proud of them, and that's the highest praise I can give. . . . I can't tell you how awful it was. The sheer, barren loneliness. . . . Somehow they managed to isolate us, so that we were just two freaks in a world which had all its lists made up already, and simply hadn't a place left for freaks. So they pretended that we weren't there. You know what we became, in the end? *Nothing!* We didn't exist except as a joke, and even then no one saw the joke.

'I mean that literally,' he continued. 'When we went to a party, not only did we never talk to anybody, we never met a single pair of eyes. We simply weren't there! Even the waiters used to hand us our drinks as if they were passing them through a curtain. Once I heard a man say: "Smith and Jones? Are they still around? I always mix them up with the Dolly Sisters."' His burning eyes, from which the tears were already starting, glared at me, daring me to laugh. Then he sighed, deeply. 'And yet, you know, I still prefer this country. I still think it's more hopeful, I still think it has better answers for the future. It just so happened that they couldn't find a place for us, at this stage.' He drew another deep breath. 'And all I wanted to do was create.'

'You could have done that at home,' I said. 'With a little more patience. Maybe a little more guts. We *are* creating, and you are one of us.'

'We were not creating. We were manufacturing. Anyway, I was never "one of us". I was me.' I noticed that he had slipped, ominously, into the past tense, as if a certain stage had been reached, and he could now survey his life, and mine, as part of disappearing history. The effect was heightened when he said: 'Water over the dam, anyway. . . . Old sad songs. . . . We come now to the matter in hand.'

At that, he turned his attention, not to me but to

the bottle, as if it were some kind of hour-glass—as perhaps for him it was; the amount of whisky remaining might be his measurement of life—my life, or his. The fanciful thought, prompted by this insane session, remained with me as he reached for a glass which stood by the water carafe on my desk, and carefully poured a fresh drink—about half what was left. As he drank it, his eyes above the rim of the glass regained that look of calculation I had noticed before, and then seemed to pass on to another stage. The calculation took a turn for the worse, into anger, into hatred. . . . I had forgotten, until then, that he was fresh from murder; now he looked it, clearly, transparently, and he indicated his new target when he drained the glass, with a toss of his head, and said: 'The matter in hand is you.'

I looked at him, I looked at the revolver. They were both too far away, for anything I could do. I said:

'What about me?'

'Don't rush me. I might change my mind.' He was frowning now, really concentrating. 'I thought of killing you,' he said. 'It would have been one of those rare pleasures, like hitting a child on Christmas morning.' I could not guess whether he had been the grown-up, or the child, or the onlooker, on whatever day this was which still lived and burned; or whether he were joking, or showing off, or babbling. 'But there's a better way. It's better, because it involves the maximum damage to all the things I detest.'

He was so sure of himself, so calmly malevolent, that I could not feel relief. The axe was still poised. 'Why did you want to kill me?'

'For the same reason as I'm going to jump out of that window.' He jerked his head back, to one of the two windows behind him. 'Because I loathe you, and all you stand for, and this will hurt you far more than anything else I could do. It's as easy as that, Drill-Pig. If I kill you, I release you. If I do it this way, you're going to sweat blood for the rest of your life.'

'I would doubt that.'

'You won't, when it happens. . . . Do you think people will believe it's suicide? The death of Jones, as well as Smith, within forty-eight hours? Jones falling from a window *in our own Embassy*? Where he was being kept prisoner?' He laughed wildly. 'Be your age! It'll be taken for granted as an official murder, for revenge, by you people. Probably by you! You'll be lucky if you get a job as janitor in the Security building, after this comes out. And that's about all you'll be good for, Drill-Pig.'

I did not need to think for more than ten seconds to know that he spoke the truth. This was the trump card he had been storing up, scheming to play. Smith murdered, Jones pushed out of an Embassy window, or jumping to escape torture; it could only be put down to our account, and I would be the only one to pay it. Jones was right; my career, if not my life, would come to a dead stop, from the moment it happened; and Jones had the whip hand.

I asked him again, the question I truly did not understand. 'But why do you want to do this to me?'

'Because I hate you, Drill-Pig.' He did not need to hesitate for answers; he had a map of his world spread out before him. 'You just can't believe that, can you? Well, it's true.' He was staring at me, a small, ferociously loathing man. 'I see in you all that is wrong with my country, all that makes it so despicable. I would do anything to hurt it, and anything to hurt you. But if I'd thought and planned for twenty years, I still couldn't have dreamed up a better way than this.'

His hand was reaching for the bottle, the bottle with the last full drink in it. It rattled against the rim of the glass as he poured half of it out, and hearing it he smiled inanely. 'Sounds my mother taught me,' he said. '*My* music.' He raised the glass, and took his first gulp.

It seemed I did not have much time; he might be half drunk, or mad, or eaten up with hatred, but the effect was going to be the same. I could only plunge right in, with my own trump cards, such as they were.

'I'll do a deal with you,' I said. 'I have full authority. You can pretty well name your own price.'

'Deal?' He was squinting, a sort of caricature of a drunk man trying to understand; not a very good one. 'What sort of deal?'

'If you'll stop right now,' I said, 'and come back to us, you can have a hundred thousand dollars in cash, and a job when you get home. Or we'll give you a plane ticket to any neutral country you like, and a permanent pension when you get there. If you'll just say "Yes" to either of those, I'll leave you here, and come back on Monday with an irrevocable guarantee, a cashier's cheque on the Embassy's own bank.'

I had thought to surprise him, even to take his breath away. But it did not work like that; he was too far gone in drink, or in hatred, or despair, for the proposition to touch him. A strange look came over his face, a momentary puzzlement; that was all the reaction I had.

'Am I so important?' he muttered, almost to himself.

'We think so.'

'I used not to be.'

I smiled, as convincingly as I could. 'That was yesterday. . . . How about it?'

By way of answer he poured out the very last of the whisky, and drank it methodically, sip by sip, until the glass was drained. Then he shook his head from side to side, slowly, and put his hands down, one on the desk, one on the revolver, and began to rise.

'It's too late.' he said. 'You should have thought of that ten years ago. . . . I wouldn't take a golden pyramid from you now. . . . Now I haven't any choice.'

He edged back to the nearest window, covering me with the revolver; he moved stiffly, like a little old man with a boy's debauched face. He had trouble with the window-catch, because he was watching me all the time; finally he levered up the sash, painfully, with one hand, and the gaping space stood waiting for his exit.

'Two hundred thousand,' I said. The open window let in a waft of icy air, straight off the frozen river, but I was sweating nonetheless. 'Don't do it. It's not worth it.'

'It's worth it,' he answered. He gestured with the revolver towards the other window. 'Take a look out, and you'll see why it's worth it. We have company, Drill-Pig. Your friends are waiting for me.'

I crossed swiftly to the window, and looked down. The view was onto the street, gleaming white in the morning sunlight. There were no passers-by; there were only loiterers—I counted four of them—at strategic corners of the building. One of them, black-coated, chanced to be looking up; when he saw me at the window, he turned away again, and stared fixedly in the opposite direction.

'They know I'm here,' said Jones. His voice was trembling, and he made an enormous effort to master it. 'They know you're here with me. But they're not coming in. They're waiting for me to come out.'

I knew that he spoke, once more, the fatal truth. The waiting men were to be the witnesses. I could even forecast what they would say; that Jones had appeared at a window on the top floor of our Embassy, that he was struggling, that he appeared to be impelled outwards, that he fell to his death while an impassive compatriot watched him drop. . . . There would be blood on the snow after all. . . . Other newspapers might put the word 'suicide' in quotes: it would be made clear that we had kidnapped Jones, perhaps tortured him and driven him insane. But whatever the version, our guilt would be monstrously clear. In one way or another, it would be an execution.

Major Tollman would not help me now. The winning hand had been dealt to him; he must have traced Jones by the phone call from the Embassy, but he was leaving the rest of the story to me, because I had walked into a simple trap and he need not even spring it. Tollman would win this one, after all, as he had doubtless been planning to all along.

I remembered him saying: 'We would be glad to see you all in hell.' Very soon, in a small way, he was going to begin to be glad.

Jones was astride the window-sill already. He was trembling more violently, and his face was working in a series of frightful grimaces; but the revolver still covered me, and I was powerless. The watchers below had given up their pretence, and were staring, open-mouthed, at the poised figure.

Jones inched outwards very slowly. He said, in a shaking voice: 'This isn't so easy after all. . . . I wanted to die drunk, and I'm not. I'm terribly sober. . . . But I will still do it.'

It was the first time I had ever heard him sound like a Russian.

I sprang forward at the last second, but he had already dropped the revolver, and leaned sideways, and toppled over. A terrible feeling of bereavement, the first of my life, took hold of me as I watched him go. He screamed and flailed his arms wildly as he fell, far from his home and from mine, in the heart of that strange, far-away foreign capital—Ottawa.